'Love?'

Brett cut in me
woman, want *love*

He released Lauren so suddenly that the room spun. This was a side to him she had never seen, never guessed at.

'I—I *hate* you like this. What happened while you were away that you've lost your human warmth? I wouldn't make love with you if—if—'

'If I *paid* you?' Brett added insultingly.

'The man who arrived on the doorstep that night wouldn't have said that. You've changed from the man I knew, the man I liked.'

'Oh, no, Lauren. You never knew me.'

Lilian Peake grew up in Essex. Her first job was working for a writer of mystery stories. Subsequently she bacame a journalist on a provincial newspaper, then moved to a trade magazine and reported on fashion. Later she took on an advice column in a women's magazine. She began writing romances because she loves happy endings! She lives near Oxford, England, with her husband, a retired college principal. They have two sons, a daughter and two grandsons. Her hobbies are walking, reading and listening to classical music.

CARMICHAEL'S RETURN

BY
LILIAN PEAKE

MILLS & BOON

*MILLS & BOON and the Rose Device
are trademarks of the publisher.
Harlequin Mills & Boon Limited,
Eton House, 18–24 Paradise Road, Richmond, Surrey TW9 1SR*

© Lilian Peake 1996

ISBN 0 263 79742 2

*Set in 10 on 10½ pt Linotron Times
01-9610-58458*

*Typeset in Great Britain by CentraCet, Cambridge
Made and printed in Great Britain*

CHAPTER ONE

LAUREN made herself more comfortable in the chair next to the telephone. Her friend Marie's calls were always long—especially this one as they hadn't met since Marie had moved house.

'Please,' Marie coaxed into Lauren's ear, 'think about it. For Reggie's sake as well as mine. If you loved your boyfriend as much as I love Reggie... OK,' she added hurriedly, 'so yours ditched you—'

'Other way round,' Lauren supplied without rancour.

'Oops, sorry. You ditched Mitch. I'd ditch Reggie too if he played around with other girls. Anyway, I can't let Reggie go and work in France without me just because I took on the job my uncle offered me before Reggie knew about being transferred to the Continent. He's starting his job next week,' she added on a note of anguish.

'But Marie, you haven't been there long. How can you move out so soon after agreeing to live there? Anyway, I've never house-sat, or whatever you call it.'

'Lauren—' Marie's voice came pleadingly '—Uncle Redmund doesn't want the place left empty, that's all. He doesn't want to sell it, he wants someone occupying it. By the way, he's not my real uncle. He's a very old friend of my parents. I've called him Uncle since I was a kid. Oh, and I did mention, didn't I, that he's currently living in the South of France? And as for moving away from here so quickly—well, it's how things happen, isn't it?'

'Maybe, but—'

'There's a salary attached to it—a substantial one. You'll agree to house-sit, then?' Marie pleaded.

'I didn't say so.'

'But you'll need to look for another place to live;
you told me so,' Marie countered. 'Your landlord's
decided to sell the house and—'

'OK, that's true, but I'll still need to think about
what you've suggested. I'm on an art agency's books
for work—'

'So withdraw your name,' Marie urged. 'A job's
being offered you right now. Look,' she went on, as her
friend still seemed to be hesitating, 'I'm giving a party
Saturday evening at Uncle Redmund's house to celebrate Reggie's promotion—because that's what it is.
Come to it, Lauren.'

'Well, I—'

'You could come Friday and stay overnight,' Marie
suggested. 'That way you could really get the feel of
the place. I'll show you round and you can give me
your answer then. Oh—and this is not blackmail or
anything—but there's a job vacancy for me over there
in Reggie's office. Won't that be just great? That is, if
I'm able to join him.'

'If that's *not* blackmail then my name's not Lauren
Halstead,' Lauren protested, making a face at her
friend's laughter.

'Maybe kind of, then,' Marie conceded. 'See you
Friday, yes? And don't worry about help in bringing
your things here. Reggie can hire a van to bring any
heavy furniture over.'

'There's only lightweight stuff,' Lauren answered.
Then she realised she was already in the process of
committing herself. 'But, Marie,' she added hastily, 'I
haven't said yes, have I?'

'Do you think I'd let a little thing like that stand in
my way?' was her friend's laughing riposte.

Marie called for Lauren in the small car her 'uncle'
Redmund had provided for her while she looked after
his property.

'This car will be yours to use while you're staying

here,' Marie declared, silencing any protest Lauren
might have made about not yet having come to a
decision by swinging across the road and pulling up in
the drive.

The outside of the house had an unmistakable charm.
It was stone-built, with bay windows below and sash
windows to the bedrooms on the upper floor. It had
more length than height, and something in it reached
out to the artist in Lauren.

'It's been added to over the centuries,' Marie
explained as she joined Lauren on the gravelled driveway. 'It's nearly three hundred years old. Come on in.'

The living area was so large it almost took Lauren's
breath away. Oak beams had been left in place, inset
into the ceiling, while the stone fireplace, which had
been cleverly restored, occupied a large area of wall,
with alcoves left for ornaments and even books.

'Three rooms were knocked into one,' Marie
explained, arms swinging wide. 'And this is the
kitchen—' she led the way '—all mod cons. Everything
a girl could ever want. Yes?' She looked coaxingly into
Lauren's face.

Lauren could only nod, but quickly qualified the
action with a noncommittal, 'Maybe.'

'And upstairs,' Marie went on, and the staircase
creaked as they went up, 'there are so many bedrooms
you could almost sleep in a different one every night.
All with *en suite* facilities, as they say in hotel bro-
chures. How's that for modernity? And here—' she
flung a door wide '—you could paint and draw to your
heart's content. It used to be Uncle Redmund's study.
Yes?' she repeated, smiling winningly.

'Mmm,' was all Lauren was prepared to say at that
moment, but the sound prolonged itself into an appreci-
ative affirmative.

Inside, she could feel all opposition to the whole idea
melting. In that room, in which there was virtually no
furniture, the light from the huge floor-to-ceiling win-

dows—plus the two skylights that had been inserted
into the sloping roof—was so good that she knew at
once how easily she could work there.

On their way down Lauren commented on the oil
paintings which adorned the staircase walls and
hallway.

'Paintings acquired by Uncle Redmund. They're
quite valuable, by the way.' She paused, pointing to
three empty picture hooks. 'Here hung Mrs Redmund
Gard the first, and here Mrs Redmund Gard the
second.'

'This one?' Lauren asked.

'And on this one, Uncle Redmund's son. The bad
boy of the family, or so the story goes.'

They had reached the hallway. 'So what happened?'
Lauren prompted.

'Well. . .' Counting on her fingers, Marie told her.
'Mrs Gard the first left him. Mrs Gard the second
likewise, and—'

'Don't tell me, the bad son left him too?'

'He did. Uncle Redmund—or so my parents told
me—accused his son of having an affair with his
stepmother and driving her away from him. Said son
had a furious row with his father, denying the accu-
sation, but his father didn't believe him.'

'Threw him out?'

'Either that or the probably guilty son fled the nest.
In other words, he upped and left, never to be heard of
or from again.'

'What a strange story,' Lauren commented sadly.

Marie nodded. 'The Press got hold of it, so paternal
parent took full advantage of the publicity and told the
world of his son's many other amorous exploits. Thus
clearing himself of the suggestion of having falsely
accused his son of stealing his second wife's affections,
as Uncle Redmund so dramatically put it.'

'Hence the three empty picture hooks,' Lauren
supplied.

'Yep. Did I tell you,' Marie asked as they entered the living room, 'that tomorrow night's get-together is going to be a kind of farewell party? Reggie and I are leaving the next morning.'

'Which means I'd be in charge from then on?'

Marie nodded, frowning. 'Do you mind, Lauren? I mean, if you do. . .'

'You'd have to stay here,' Lauren took her up with a wry smile, 'losing your chance of that job in Reggie's firm and crying your heart out while he gets on with his life across the Channel *without you*?'

'I was going to say I'd have to find someone else to live here,' Marie responded pleadingly, but with the light of hope in her eyes. 'Although there's nobody around I could possibly trust like I trust you.'

Lauren smiled. 'Flattery will get you everywhere. Oh, Marie—' she hugged her friend '—you know I'll do it, don't you?'

At which, Marie laughed, gave her friend a hug in return, then dashed off to call the caterers.

Glancing through the living room window, Lauren felt the pull of the gardens, and, pushing open the glass-paned doors, she took a deep breath of country air and went to explore.

There were paved paths winding round, bordered by beds planted with sweet-smelling flowers and varied shrubs. In the centre of the main lawn stood a cedar tree, its branches wide-spreading, throwing shadows over the stone-walled residence.

In various places throughout the extensive gardens there were terracotta heads poised on short columns. Lauren ran her hand over them, appreciating the skill of the artist. Studying them more closely, she began to wonder who the people were that they represented.

Her artist's eye picked up details that were common to them all—the delicacy of the features, the strong nose, the jaw-line, the well-shaped lips. In all of them, however, the eyes were blank, telling her nothing.

Back inside, Lauren paused in the doorway to the living area, admiring the view once more. The sun had moved round and the flowers' colours glowed just as brilliantly but from a different angle.

The great cedar tree placed centrally in the lawn now flung its huge shadow right across her body. She had the strangest feeling of being both pushed away by its far-reaching branches and yet drawn in, as if they were great arms pulling her towards them.

Although there was no hint of a breeze in the still air, a shiver coursed through her.

Late on the day before, after explaining the where-abouts of the various keys to the property, and all the other details a house-sitter needed to know, Marie had shown Lauren to the guest room.

It was a low-ceilinged, chintz-curtained hideaway, with dark wooden furniture and a worn carpet half hidden by rugs.

And now, minutes before joining the party, Lauren studied her reflection in the long mirror as she combed her deep brown hair, draping it to curl each side of her oval-shaped face. A curiously excited, pre-party mood enveloped her, even though her only friend amongst the partygoers would be Marie—plus, of course, Reggie, Marie's fiancé. She placed a light layer of lipstick on her full lips, but her eyes, grey and winsome, she did not touch.

'They're so dreamy,' Mitch had told her after a few dates. 'A guy could lose himself in those eyes of yours. Plus they make a guy wonder just where he stands with you.'

'"Stand" is the right word,' Lauren had smilingly retorted.

'Is that a challenge?' Mitch had asked, and had not believed her when she had nodded.

He had grown angry and told her that if she didn't let her barriers down soon he'd *make* her. . . At which she had told him coolly that rape was a criminal offence and that as she wasn't victim material she didn't want to date him any more. At that point he had stormed from her digs and she had never heard from him again.

What can I do, she asked her reflection now, to give those eyes a down-to-earth look? Making a few faces at herself, she laughed and gave up trying. Fixing a choker of hand-turned polished wooden beads to follow the neckline of her black and white striped cotton top, she smoothed the well-fitting fabric into the waistband of her black velvet trousers, then ran the comb once more through her long hair.

That morning Reggie, Marie's fiancé, had called for Lauren, and helped load her belongings into the hired van.

'My promotion's going to put some extra cash into my bank account,' he had confided as he drove. 'Which means a better car when I take up my job. Better everything, in fact.' His head had turned towards Lauren, then quickly back again. 'I can't say how pleased I am, Lauren, that you've agreed to take over from Marie. I—' He had laughed, a little embarrassed. 'It would have broken my heart to leave her behind.'

Lauren sighed inwardly. Lucky them, she thought, to have fallen equally hard for each other, to be so sure of each other's love.

Leaning out of the wondow, Lauren watched Marie welcoming her guests, who were now arriving in droves.

Descending the stairs a little later, she noted that Marie and Reggie were busy mingling. Marie turned and saw her friend. 'Feel free,' she mouthed, 'to wander and inspect again.'

The increasing volume of sound faded as Lauren took Marie at her word. At the end of her journey of discovery Lauren came to the conclusion that it would be a delightful place to live. But alone? She wasn't so sure.

'This place just goes on and on,' she commented to

Marie as she inspected the buffet-type meal which the caterers had set out in the farmhouse-style kitchen.

'Once it was three separate cottages,' Marie explained. 'Through the years they've been joined together, and Old Cedar Grange is the result.'

Lauren frowned. 'I don't know how I'll feel, Marie, living here alone.'

'But, Lauren,' Marie responded, 'I've been on my own in this place for nearly two months now. That is—' she coloured just a little '—when Reggie hasn't been with me.'

'There you are, then,' Lauren took her up. 'You weren't alone, were you?'

'So get yourself a boyfriend,' Reggie joined in the discussion from the kitchen door, 'and invite him to stay here too.'

'She ditched Mitch,' Marie pointed out, at which they all laughed.

By now the volume of sound had risen considerably, with the arrival of the friends with the hi-fi equipment.

It was a good thing, Lauren thought a few hours later, her ears tiring of the music, her muscles weary from the dancing, that Marie's uncle's house stood surrounded by its own grounds, well away from its neighbours. Otherwise, she reflected, complaints would have arrived by the dozen via the telephone, and maybe even in the form of remonstrating policemen on the doorstep.

The living room windows had been flung wide, the doors to the garden likewise. The long, undrawn brown velvet curtains billowed in the breeze, while the spotlights on the patio illuminated the surrounding shrubbery.

'Want to share?' A young man who had introduced himself as Casey Talbert offered his overflowing plate to Lauren.

She shook her head and wondered how soon she could slip upstairs to her room. She wondered also how she could put a distance between herself and this persistent guest called Casey. For most of the evening he had followed her about.

The music had grown louder, the beat more insistent. Casey, seemingly unable to resist its call, put aside his plate and pulled Lauren into the midst of the twisting, whirling crowd.

She looked around for Marie, hoping to be able to break free of Casey and explain to her that she was tired and was going to bed, but there was no sign of her. Nor could she see Reggie anywhere.

'If you're looking for our host and hostess,' Casey shouted over the din, inventing his own arms-and-legs mode of dancing, 'I saw them get into Reggie's car.'

'Gone for more supplies, probably,' a girl beside him hazarded.

The telephone shrilled demandingly over the music and the laughter.

'Hi, Lauren.' Marie's voice came brightly through the receiver. 'Find a chair. This might come as a shock. We're on our way to the coast.'

'Wh-why?' Lauren stuttered. 'I mean. . .supplies— you were going to get more s-supplies, or so I heard.'

'Just a red herring, Lauren.' Marie sounded apologetic now. 'We thought we'd make our getaway while the party was in full swing, without waiting for the morning. Say goodbye to everyone, will you? And barrowloads of thanks for their prezzies.'

'But all your things—' was all Lauren could get out.

'Packed them secretly this afternoon in the hired van, after Reggie unloaded yours. Sorry it was so sudden, Lauren, but, as I said, we thought we'd make a dash before—'

'Before I changed my mind?' Lauren retorted, but with a smile in her voice.

'We—ell, maybe. We're crossing in the morning to house-hunt. Giving ourselves a day or two free before Reggie's job starts.'

'So this is it,' Lauren said. 'From now on I take responsibility for your Uncle Redmund's house?'

'Until we get back, yep,' Marie replied brightly.

'Which is—?'

'Can't really say—' Marie began, then Reggie took over.

'Sorry, Lauren, to drop you in it like this, but I—we—were desperate. If you'd decided in the end to say no—'

Lauren sighed loudly. 'OK, so I was set up. But as it was by my best friend, and my best friend's fiancé, I guess I'll have to count my blessings. I've got a job. I've got a roof—and what a roof!—over my head. I can't really grumble, can I?'

She smiled at the prolonged sigh of relief from the other end.

'By the way, before I go,' Marie added, 'a word of warning about Casey Talbert. He might have been playing the complete idiot this evening, but he's no fool. He can't be, otherwise he couldn't hold down his job as a reporter on the local paper. He graduated from his journalists' course a few months ago, and as you can probably imagine he's panting to make his mark as an ace reporter. His nose is very firmly to the ground, Lauren, whether it's clean down there, or not—if you get my meaning?'

'I get it,' Lauren answered.

'Good. Thought I'd better warn you. Cheers. We'll be in touch,' Marie declared, just before the phone went dead.

A high-pitched scream came from the direction of one of the windows. Hand shaking a little, Lauren went to pick up the phone again, then realised she had no number on which to call Marie back.

'There's a man in the garden,' a young woman shrieked. 'No, he's not one of us,' she shouted, contradicting someone's suggestion. 'He's acting strange. Oh, no, he's coming this way.' She screamed again. 'He might have a gun!'

'She's been watching too many films,' Casey said, then joined the general lurch towards the patio doors, pulling Lauren with him. 'Can't miss this.'

They were pushed by the crush through the doors, white garden table and chairs being overturned on the way, and Lauren emerged dishevelled and breathless to see the dark shape of a man standing, hands on hips, at the edge of the paving stones.

'Everyone take cover!' someone shouted, screams following his command. 'For Pete's sake, where's Marie? Where's Reggie? Can't they get rid of the guy?'

'They've gone!' Lauren cried. 'To France.'

'You must be joking,' was the strangled answer from the depths of the crowd.

Lauren had been pulled into a crouching position beside Casey, who in turn was crouching behind the toppled table, but, like a soldier in a war zone, he kept his eager eyes just above the parapet.

It came to her with some force that as she had now become the official house-sitter it was for her to take the lead and remonstrate with the interloper, persuade him to go on his way.

She tugged her hand from Casey's.

'Where are you going?' he croaked.

'To get rid of the gatecrasher.' She stood up and picked her way through cowering bodies. A gasp went up at her audacity, her foolhardy bravery.

'He might have a gun!' Casey repeated the warning, having plainly cast aside his mockery of the girl who had first uttered it.

'So what?' Lauren threw over her shoulder, sounding far more confident than she really felt. Because of the darkness no one could see how her hands were shaking. Nor could they hear her racing heartbeats, nor know how dry her mouth had become.

The others made a gangway, gazing up at her with

admiration mixed with fear for her safety. She needed to walk some distance—to her inflamed imagination it seemed a safari trek—to confront the interloper.

He stood beneath the tree—that tree which the day before had stretched out its arms towards her. She knew now that it had not been repelling her, but drawing her nearer and nearer. And nearer still to the darkly threatening figure of the stranger who lurked in its shadows. Then she was in front of him, wishing she could stop her heartbeats from shaking her whole being.

He was so tall she had to tilt her head to search his face, but his features were in shadow, the lights from the house only illuminating his body from the chest down.

His arms were folded, his shoulder supported by the trunk of the tree. His long legs were crossed indolently at the ankles and a heavy backpack, which had plainly just been shrugged off, was lying beside him.

Lauren's eyes dropped involuntarily to his hips, looking at his pockets.

'I have no gun.'

So he'd heard the warning shouts. His statement had come tonelessly and Lauren found herself believing him, although why, she did not know.

His hands came out and her heart nearly jumped into her throat. 'I have these.' The words came softly from the semi-darkness. 'But I use them to caress a woman, not to harm her.'

'Will you please go?' Her voice sounded hoarse, and she clasped her hands in front of her to hide their trembling. 'This is a private party on private property.'

Eyes staring, she watched as his hand went again to a pocket, but she relaxed as he drew out a handkerchief. Her gaze followed its path to his forehead from which, to her puzzlement and surprise, he seemed to mop perspiration. The night-time air was cool, so his action could surely only mean that he, too, was afraid. *Of her?*

As he replaced the handkerchief his hand seemed to shake, yet to Lauren, staring at him in the semi-darkness, his whole demeanour seemed to be one of self-assurance verging on arrogance.

There was a long silence while he sized her up, taking in her striped, close-fitting top, the velvet trousers over her shapeliness, up and up, to take in her face, her hair, her lips. Cheeks burning, she almost felt his piercing regard.

She wished she could see him, read his expression, judge his character by the look in his eyes, but the shadows still swallowed him from his shoulders upwards.

'I belong. . .'

It was almost as though he couldn't finish the sentence. His tone had changed. The words had come in a hoarse whisper.

There was a shuffling sound from behind her, and she wondered whether the others were moving nearer to protect her or withdrawing into the interior. Music from the living room told her that the guests had decided the stranger was either an acquaintance or harmless. She had half turned to see how many were left outside when another sound had her turning back.

The stranger was bending with obvious difficulty to retrieve his backpack, swinging it into position. The effort must have cost him dear, since he dropped it, following it down and crumpling to the ground. As he fell his head thumped against the tree trunk, and he lay motionless, scarcely breathing, at Lauren's feet.

CHAPTER TWO

'No!' LAUREN heard her own voice cry out. She dropped to his side and felt the dampness of his forehead beneath her trembling palm.

So it had been illness, not fear which had made him dab at his brow. With features such as his, how could she have thought this man lacked courage? But then, in the darkness she had not seen the strong lines in his face, hinting at an inbuilt resolve; the full, sensual mouth that suggested powerful feelings; the jaw telling of an ability to curb those feelings, keep them under control.

A lock of damp hair hung over his forehead and Lauren watched her quivering fingers push it aside. I've seen this man before. . . The words hit her like a lightning-strike, flashing in then out of her mind. It was a stupid thought. She had never seen him in her life before.

Hand to his cheek, she realised how shallow his breathing had become, which meant that positive action had become imperative. He needed medical attention. But most of all—and never mind that he was a complete stranger and had been concealing himself in the shadows—at that moment he needed a bed.

'Johnny, Marty. . .' She dredged up the names of some of the guests, but the music drowned her words. 'Help me—I need help. . .'

Desperately she turned her head, seeing one figure lingering outside. She might as well, she thought, make use of the dog-like devotion the young man had been displaying towards her all evening.

'Casey!' she yelled. '*Casey!* Help me.' To her relief

he moved towards her. 'Help me lift this man—get him inside.'

Casey, nearer now, took one look then dashed back, shouting, 'Johnny!' and gesturing wildly. Johnny came, following Casey across the patio, thudding over the lawn and pulling up smartly at the sight of the recumbent figure.

'What's wrong with him?' Johnny panted, hands on hips. 'Is he dead?'

'He fainted—can't you see?' Casey rebuked him, his slightly cloying manner vanished. 'Now, how can we do this?'

Casey Talbert sober, Lauren decided, was a great improvement on Casey Talbert intoxicated.

'You take his feet, Johnny,' Casey directed, 'while I carry him like this.' He fitted his hands beneath the stranger's armpits and prepared to lift him, but found himself holding a twisting torso.

'For God's sake—' the words came hoarsely from the man '—I can walk.'

Shaking his head, as if to get his brain working again, and with a massive effort, the stranger got himself to his feet, swaying as he struggled to stay upright. Impulsively Lauren flung her arms around his waist, taking his weight with her own body. She staggered back, and felt him try to help her by easing himself away, but she managed to hold him more firmly.

'Come on, Lauren,' Casey urged. 'Let me walk him into the house. If that's—?'

Lauren nodded vigorously. 'Where else? In this state he'll not make it to his car. If he's got a car.' All the same, her arms still clung, seemingly strangely reluctant to let him go.

'OK, Lauren,' said Johnny, 'let us take over.'

Slowly Lauren detached herself from the stranger, feeling a curious emptiness inside her as her body lost contact with his. She tried lifting his backpack, but found it so heavy she had to drag it over the lawn.

The man did his best to co-operate as they walked him, his legs lifting heavily with each step, but his head stayed determinedly upright, although Lauren guessed its natural inclination must be to hang.

'Through the kitchen,' Lauren directed, but the two men were making for the easiest way in, which was through the open doorway into the living room.

Someone turned down the music, and guests pulled aside to make a passage through. Eyes stared, hands holding glasses stilled on their way to open mouths.

Casey and Johnny made for the stairs, Casey calling over his shoulder, 'OK, folks. Party's over. No one to see off. Marie and Reggie have gone. Thanks on their behalf for coming.'

As the three men slowly mounted the stairs, the stranger's feet dragging just a little, the music was switched off, shouts of farewell rang out and car doors slammed.

'Thanks, Lauren.' A girl reached Lauren's side on the wide stairs, helping her bump the backpack upwards. 'You did a great stand-in job on our absent hostess's behalf.' She added after a pause, 'You're doing a fine Samaritan act too—more than I'd do for a total stranger skulking in the shadows. Good luck. I've a feeling you'll need it. We're all going home.'

She ran downstairs and the door slammed behind her.

Lauren was thankful that the house possessed so many bedrooms—two or three of which, she had noticed during her inspection of the place, were already made up for possible guests. Friends, no doubt, of Marie's.

At Lauren's request Casey and Johnny had taken the man to the room next to hers. They'd removed his outer clothing, leaving his jeans in place, his shirt unbuttoned.

Lauren lifted the cover over him, noticing that the strong, lean body appeared to be deeply tanned.

'He couldn't have got that toasted from the sun in this country,' Johnny commented quietly. 'Must have been in the tropics for some while, I'd guess.'

'So what brought him here?' Casey said, voice low. 'Homing instinct?'

'*Homing?*' Lauren exclaimed. 'He doesn't live here. No connection with the place—otherwise Marie would have told me.' Then she remembered the man's muttered half-sentence—'I belong. . .'

He must have meant this country, she decided, recalling that the few words he had spoken had told her that his accent seemed to be British in origin. If he had indeed been roaming the world for a while, he would refer to his connection with his native country as 'belonging' to it, wouldn't he?

'Johnny!' yelled a girl's voice from below. 'Come and drive us home like you promised.'

Complying with the good-humoured command, Johnny paused at the door. 'He's a good-looking guy, Lauren. Don't you go falling for him.' Lifting his hand in acknowledgement of Lauren's thanks, he went on his way.

'He won't be here that long,' Lauren declared.

'Anyway, he's probably married with half a dozen kids,' commented Casey. 'With looks like that some female must have snapped him up years ago.'

'How old do you think he is?' whispered Lauren. 'I'd say—thirty-five?'

'Could be,' said Casey uninterestedly. He gestured her outside to the corridor.

'Look, Lauren, I know we only met this evening, but I have to say sorry about my infantile behaviour at the party. I'd had more to drink than I'm used to. I do like you, honest.' His smile, head on one side, melted away her irritation with him, then his face straightened. 'And it worries me, you being alone with this guy from nowhere. I could stay a few hours, if you like, until he's come round and been able to establish his identity?'

Lauren hesitated. The thought had been worrying her too. She'd told Marie that she might not enjoy being alone in the house, but she hadn't bargained for such a mysterious companion.

Wouldn't 'intruder' be a better word? her subconscious prompted. Had the dramatic collapse under the tree been one big act, a way of getting a bed for the night? After all, his surface appearance seemed dishevelled, and his backpack showed distinct signs of wear.

Lauren lifted her shoulders, returning to gaze down at the stranger. The half-light illuminated the planes and angles of his face, the lines from nose to mouth, the frown marks between his eyes. The jaw, around which was a considerable growth of stubble, was resolute, the forehead wide, only the hair still damp from perspiration, resisting the downward droop of his demeanour and curling into itself.

There was something in those features that was vaguely familiar, although for the life of her Lauren couldn't recall ever having met him, or even having seen his photograph anywhere. She didn't know why, but instinctively she felt it was a face she could trust.

'I'll be OK,' she said softly to Casey. 'It'll only be for one night, after all. Tomorrow he'll probably go on his way. Wherever that might be.'

'We—ell. . .' Casey was only partly reassured. 'Could be he's suffering from a mega-sized hangover.'

Lauren half agreed, although there had been no hint of alcohol on his breath.

In the dim light she gazed at the stranger. He appeared to be asleep. As she stared there arose inside her not even a trace of fear of him. If there had been any reason to be afraid of this man, surely her instinct would have told her, not letting her rest until at the very least she'd called the police?

'I'll be OK,' she assured Casey again. 'But thanks a lot for your offer.'

'I'll write down my phone number.' He scribbed on

a piece of paper from his pocket. 'If you have any doubts about him at all, you can reach me here, at my digs. Only twenty minutes' drive. Any time, remember, Lauren.'

On impulse, she did something that half an hour ago she would never have dreamt of doing where Casey was concerned. She reached up and kissed his cheek.

'Thanks a lot,' she said, and watched him colour with pleasure.

He wasn't slow. He put his arms around her and placed a hard kiss against her lips, then lifted his hand as he left, whistling as he pounded down the stairs.

In the bedroom, Lauren wiped her mouth with the back of her hand and stared down at the backpack. If she looked inside, it would be a way, wouldn't it, of discovering *something* about the man?

There was no discernible movement from him, so she found her flashlight and crouched down, unfastening straps, opening flaps and peering into the interior. There was a pocket tape-recorder, notebooks and pencils, lightweight clothes, plastic containers which rattled, envelopes containing letters. Eagerly she turned the beam of light onto the name of the addressee.

'Brett Carmichael', it read, 'c/o PO Box No. . .'

The destination appeared to be somewhere in Africa. At least she had discovered his name, if not his mission.

It seemed that Johnny had been right in his guess that to acquire such a tan the man must have been in the tropics. So what were the events that had caused him to show up out of the blue—or, more correctly, she thought, out of the darkness—on the doorstep of Old Cedar Grange?

The bedclothes rustled and Lauren hurried to the stranger's side. His eyes fluttered open, moving around as if he was trying to work out where he was. What was he thinking? Lauren wondered. Which room am I in— which dwelling—which country? Or even, for a man as good-looking as he was, Whose bedroom this time? Then she reproached herself for prejudging him. His morals might be beyond suspicion. Perhaps he was wondering where his wife was, his family?

Lauren's heart did the strangest dive at the thought, then surfaced with speed at her silent reprimand. He meant nothing to her, this man from the shadows. How could he, when she knew nothing about him, when he'd only come into her life about thirty minutes ago?

She leaned over him and he stared up at her, fixing his brown eyes on hers, holding them as if he was truly disorientated, and clinging to their reality like a drowning person to a rock.

Summoning a smile, she smoothed back his hair. It felt damp, and there were beads of perspiration on his forehead.

'What's wrong with you?' she whispered. 'Where have you come from and why are you here?'

He did not answer, but lifted his head, and then his powerful shoulders from the bed. Was he trying to get up?

'No, no,' Lauren urged, pushing him back. 'You're ill, aren't you? You've got a fever. . .'

A fever? At least she could sponge him, couldn't she?

'Stay there,' she ordered, hoping he was receiving her. 'I won't be a moment.'

Her words must have registered as he sank back weakly, his eyes closing again. When she returned with a bowl of tepid water, facecloth and towel, his eyes were still closed. He opened them again as she wrung the cloth and mopped his brow. He appeared to be watching her every action, as if trying to comprehend the reason for her ministrations.

She pulled back the bedcover, exposing his chest and seeing the dampness there. Without hesitation she sponged the whorls of hair, a curious excitement coursing through her as she felt the muscle and the latent strength of him hard beneath her touch.

Easing back his shirt and wiping his shoulders, her wayward fingers trembled to stroke his skin, and she had to rebuke their impudence fiercely before they condescended to return to their caring mode. She used the towel to dry him.

'Name of Florence?' came the hoarse question through faintly curving lips.

'No, its L—' Then she laughed. 'No, and my surname's not Nightingale. I'm Lauren—Lauren Halstead.'

An eyebrow lifted. 'Folk in the village told me a girl called Marie lived here. Looking after the place for the absent owner.'

'That was correct until approximately an hour ago. Now I'm in charge.'

He seemed to need time to assimilate the information.

'Owner's living abroad, they said?'

'Right.'

The towel went on rubbing, moving still lower to push against his waistband. His arm swung down from his head, his hand clamping over hers. 'Oh, no, lady.'

Warmth swamped her cheeks—embarrassment mixed with anger. 'What do you take me for, Mr Carmichael?' The words burst from her as she tried to free her hand.

Beneath it, the hardness of his stomach muscles against the backs of her fingers was arousing all kinds of feelings which she had no intention of allowing to surface. They were letting her down, she fretted, fighting against her efforts to convey to him, stranger and unknown quantity that he was, that she was merely acting as an impersonal nurse and good Samaritan.

'OK, I'm sorry.' More alert now, he searched her face. 'How the hell do you know my name?'

Lauren hesitated, annoyed with herself for her give-away slip.

'OK. Stupid me. You've searched my backpack.' His shoulder lifted. 'Natural enough, in all the circumstances, for you to want to know my identity.'

Not that she did know it, she reflected. A mere name told her nothing. He released her hand and she threw the towel aside, moving to the foot of the bed and looking down at him. His head sank back onto the pillows and his eyes closed.

'Are you in pain?' she asked sympathetically.

'Yes and no. What happened to the rabble?'

'The party guests? They've gone.'

'That guy you kissed. Is he still here?'

'I was only thanking him for his help with you. And I have every right to kiss who I like.' Why was she suddenly so much on the defensive? This man, this passing stranger, merited no explanation from her. All the same, his comment implied that at the time he hadn't been totally unaware of the events going on around him.

'What kind of bug have you got?' Lauren asked. 'You collapsed outside. Did you know?'

'I knew,' he answered, so tiredly, so softly that she had to listen hard. 'It's a fever—name unpronounceable. Picked it up in my wanderings.'

She still did not know where he had 'wandered' from, or why he had chosen to 'wander' to Old Cedar Grange. But such questions, she felt, could wait until a more appropriate time. 'Should I send for a doctor?'

'No need.' He gestured towards his bag. 'I consulted a medic—of sorts. He gave me a potion. In my bag there are some tablets to deal with it. White ones. If you'd be so kind. . .' His voice tailed off.

Lauren rummaged and found them, using the flashlight to read the label. 'Take two with liquid, as required', the instructions dictated.

'I'll get some water,' she told him, and was soon back

with a glass. She put it down and shook two tablets onto her palm, then went to the bedside and held them out with the water. He managed to support himself on an elbow and dispatched the medication, swallowing and sinking back muttering, 'Thanks.'

He seemed cooler now, but plainly the fever still lingered, apparent in the flush of his cheeks, the faint layer of perspiration on his dark-shaded upper lip. His head fell to one side on the pillow, revealing the dark shadow all around his jaw. She wondered how long it was since he had shaved.

As she stared, wondering what next, he looked at her again. 'Please forgive my lack of manners. Put it down to how I feel. Nor have I thanked you for taking me in and helping to make me comfortable.' He lifted his arm, frowning at his watch. 'It's hellish late. You must be tired.'

She smiled. 'I am, but—well, that's OK.'

He nodded, lowering his lids again. For a while she stood there, studying his features anew—the wide mouth, the cleft chin, the sweeping strength of his jaw. His forehead was lined—a frown, even in sleep, creasing the skin between his eyes. There was character there, and resolution, and defiance, and surely a deep integrity?

Tiptoeing to the door, she glanced back. He had not stirred. Remembering Casey's anxiety about her being alone and defenceless with a stranger present, she withdrew the key from the inside of the door and inserted it in the lock outside, turning it and pocketing it.

She could not deny that she was just a little concerned about her situation, however much her intuition might be telling her she would be safe with this man.

A small, relieved sigh escaped her as she made for her own room, settling down at last into a deep sleep.

* * *

She was wakened by the ringing of the telephone and swung from the bed. The morning sun was lighting the room. Was it Casey, concerned for her?

Quickly cutting off the shrill ring before it woke the stranger, she answered, 'Yes?'

'May I ask who that is?' a man's voice said. 'I know it's not Marie.'

'No, I'm not Marie. And you are—?'

'My name is Redmund Gard. You are. . .Lauren— Lauren Halstead?'

'Oh, Mr Gard! Yes, I'm Lauren.' She frowned. 'How did you know?'

'Ah, now. Marie, the young minx, contacted me here in my villa in the South of France. She and her fiancé had just upped and left, it seemed, leaving a young lady bearing your name in charge of my property over there. Hoped I didn't mind, she said. To which I replied it was too bad if I did, wasn't it?'

'Oh, dear, Mr Gard. I honestly thought she'd consulted you about her intentions—although I must admit that she didn't mention that she had. If you'd rather there was someone else here instead of me, I'll advertise and—'

'No, no, my dear. She gave me a sob story of how you would soon have been made homeless.'

'That's true, but—'

'She also gave you a glowing reference—but then she would, wouldn't she?' He laughed and Lauren joined in. 'However, if you are as pleasant and intelligent as you sound, stay by all means and take care of my house. You will take over the salary I've been paying her. I hope she told you that.'

'She did, but—'

'I expect she has told you everything you need to know—about the security I had installed, the locks and bolts, not to mention the alarms?'

'Yes, she did, Mr Gard.'

'You're aware that I'm not Marie's true uncle, but

that is how she addresses me? I would like to ask you to call me Uncle Redmund too. Would you mind?'

Lauren smiled. 'Not at all—Uncle Redmund.'

'Good. By the way, today I leave on my travels again. I never stay long in one place. I suppose you could say I'm a born wanderer. The older I get, the more I want to see of this wonderful world we live in. Oh, and in an emergency—a *real* emergency only—you can contact this number.' It was a London telephone number. 'Well, goodbye for now, Lauren. And take care—of yourself, as well as my house.'

'Mr—Uncle Redmund,' she began, 'there's a man—'

He had gone.

No sooner had she replaced the receiver than there came a great hammering, followed by a series of shouts.

The stranger! Oh, heavens, she had locked him in and he had just discovered it. She raced along to his room, then remembered she had put the key in her trouser pocket.

'I'm on my way,' she yelled, and skidded back to her room, quickly returning to free him.

'For God's sake, Miss Halstead,' came a frantic voice, 'a man's gotta do what a man's gotta do.'

She burst in, quite forgetful of the fact that she hadn't had time to pull on a dressing gown and that her night attire was skimpy to say the least.

He confronted her, anger in every muscle-tough line of him, his short-sleeved shirt hanging loosely, his jeans replaced by briefs. He was pale and heavy-eyed, but it was the latent strength in his powerful maleness which triggered Lauren's femininity into responding both agitatedly and excitedly.

She had to tear her eyes away. 'I—I'm sorry. I forgot to tell you there's an *en suite*—'

'It's locked, lady. It's bloody *locked*.'

'It can't be. It—' As in the rest of the house, the bathroom lock was old-fashioned and needed a key. She tried it. He was right.

'You're not telling me you don't know where the key is?'

'Just a minute.' She dived back into her room, withdrew the key from her own bathroom lock and hopefully tried it in his. It fitted.

'Thank God for that.' He made his somewhat swaying way through the doorway.

'I'm sorry—I really didn't know.'

There was a heavy sigh, then, 'That's OK. But, Miss Halstead. . .' He eyed her minutely, assessingly, from the top of her head to her thighs, then down over her shapeliness, outlined plainly beneath the stretch fabric of her nightdress, to her tightly curling toes. 'Never— never do that to me again. . .'

Lauren fled.

Lauren stared through the kitchen window, listening to the kettle coming to the boil. The flowers glowed, the lawn radiated light. In the brilliant morning sun the cedar tree looked less intimidating, throwing its shadow away from the house.

The kitchen, as Marie had declared, possessed all the 'mod cons' a girl could want, but their modernity was in stark contrast to the roughly plastered stone walls, the oak dresser displaying blue and white crockery and the old-fashioned iron stove which had been left in place.

Should she, or shouldn't she, Lauren wondered, consult her guest about breakfast? Guest? she asked herself. Well, she could hardly think of him as 'the stranger', could she, now that she knew his name, not to mention other—well, *things* about him? The colour in her cheeks came and went at the thought.

She climbed the stairs again, but outside his room she hesitated, then her knuckles knocked tentatively on the solid wood door. She opened it on hearing a weary, 'Please enter.'

He lay back in a low chair, dressed, she noted to her

relief, in jeans and an open-necked shirt. He looked washed out.

'How are you feeling now, Mr Carmichael?'

Broad shoulders lifted and fell. 'I think the fever's passed, but I feel lousy.'

'Would you—would you like some breakfast?'

'Thanks, no.' Then his head lifted and his gaze skated with male appreciation over her casual clothes—well-washed jeans and a cotton top which, to her annoyance, no matter how baggy it became with wear, could not hide her shapeliness.

So he was OK in that specific area of his life, she thought with some amusement.

'Tea—cup of? Any chance?' he asked, letting his head fall back again.

'Of course.' She swung to the door. 'I'll go and make it.'

'Call and I'll come.'

The faintly mocking note made her turn. Fever or no fever, there was no mistaking the glint in his eyes, and her inner self cautioned, Oh, no, you don't, Mr Carmichael. Then, more insistently, Oh, no, you don't, Lauren Halstead.

CHAPTER THREE

HE DID come at her call, one slow step after the other. He dropped into an upright chair at the scrupulously scrubbed wooden table then looked around in a lacklustre way, wrapping his hands around the mug of tea which Lauren had put in front of him.

How long, she wondered, did he intend to stay? It was a question she could not yet ask of this man who, even now, was far from well.

Catching the browned bread as it jumped from the toaster, she spread it with butter and sat on the other wooden chair.

'How was it,' she asked, as much out of curiosity as to fill the taut silence, 'that you turned up in the garden of Old Cedar Grange?'

Carefully, precisely, he lowered the mug to the table, as if the movement gave him time to process his thoughts.

At last he said, 'I knocked at the front door— hammered would be a better description—but over the racket no one heard, so I did the only sensible thing and found my way to the rear.'

She nodded, chewing thoughtfully. 'But why?' She had to ask. 'Why here?'

There was another long pause. Had the fever, she wondered, slowed his mental processes? But there was no lack of brightness in his eyes, no absence of spontaneity in his reactions.

'I had a drink at the local pub,' he answered at last, 'and asked if they had any accommodation available. No room at the inn—but there was a house on the edge of the village, they told me, with plenty of empty rooms. A girl by the name of Marie Brownley lived there with her fiancé. She was looking after it in the owner's absence. They said she might put me up.'

He took a frowning mouthful of tea. He was choosing his words again. Lauren sensed it. 'Hence my appearance unannounced in the rear grounds of the property.' His mouth curved in his first real smile, and Lauren's heart lurched drunkenly at the transformation of his features.

'Totally unarmed,' he added. 'As you've no doubt discovered after going through my belongings.'

Lauren smiled too. 'Sorry about the invasion into your backpack privacy. And the "might have a gun" nonsense.'

His shoulders lifted. 'My apologies, too, for collapsing in the garden. I only flew in from South America yesterday morning. The fever, plus jet lag, caught up with me.' He straightened in the chair. It had plainly been an effort for him even to do that. 'I should leave here.' He glanced at her. 'Any chance of public transport?'

'In which direction?'

His shoulders lifted heavily. 'Any which way.'

Lauren was swept by a curious disappointment. She didn't want the man to leave, which worried her, but then she rationalised her feelings. He was company; his presence was stopping her from feeling lonely in this big house, that was all.

She was puzzled, too, by his apparent inability to make up his mind as to his eventual destination. 'I could take you to the nearest town. Where would you want to go?'

His answer was a shake of the head, a lift of the shoulders—all with his eyes closed.

'Mr Carmichael. . .' She had intended to sound firm, in order to penetrate the mists which appeared to be clouding his mind, but her voice held a strange tremor. 'You're not in a fit state to go anywhere.'

His glance at her was direct, almost speculative. He

must have heard that vocal tremor and be trying to analyse its cause. He'd be clever if he found it, she thought ruefully, because she didn't know that herself.

'You'd allow me to stay another night?'

'However long it takes for you to get well again.'

Her words surprised even herself. The statement had almost been an open invitation to stay as long as he liked. Also, her own reaction was puzzling her. It had nothing to do with the man, she told herself, with the charisma he undoubtedly possessed even in an unfit state, the magnetism in his deeply intelligent eyes, the deep-down reflex action of her feminine responses to his masculinity every time he was near.

No! It was because she was sorry for him—plainly brought low, as he was, by circumstances and illness. It was compassion, wasn't it. . .? *Wasn't it?* her brain persisted.

An eyebrow arched. 'You have it in your power to play hostess to an uninvited guest? Moreover, to someone who, twenty-four hours ago, you didn't know even existed?'

But she had known, hadn't she? Although how, she could not explain at all.

'If you mean would the owner mind if I took you in, I very much doubt it.'

'As a paying guest?'

Paying? The thought of payment hadn't occurred to her. 'Yes,' she agreed. 'Payment to the owner, not to me. I spoke to him earlier this morning and he seemed a very nice man.'

'He did? Have you ever met him?'

'How could I have? I only took over from Marie last night. Anyway, he's her uncle—or quasi-uncle.'

'Quasi.' He rolled the word around his tongue. 'I like that. Seemingly, almost, but not really.'

Lauren smiled, glad that he appeared to be reviving a little. 'You're talking like a dictionary.'

His own smile was faint. 'Dictionaries and I are on very familiar terms.'

So what was he? A teacher needing accurate interpretations? A lawyer requiring precise definitions? She didn't like to ask, and anyway it was no business of hers. Even if he stayed a while, he would leave some time in the near future. After all, he had to earn a living somehow.

Holding onto the chair, he rose carefully. 'You could be right. Maybe I'm not in a fit condition to go anywhere.' He had lost the hint of colour he'd seemed to gain from drinking the hot liquid.

'Except—' she pushed away her empty mug and stood too '—to bed.'

His lips quirked. 'My hostess is ordering me to bed? In other circumstances that might have been a promising start.'

She could not help smiling into the silence that was left as he made his way upstairs, at the same time shaking her head.

Now that he had gone, Lauren went up to the room she now regarded as her studio and attempted to bring some order to the various pieces of artists' equipment that she used in her work.

Pausing for a while, she leaned on the windowsill and gazed down into the gardens, admiring the colourful scene, her eyes drawn again to the terracotta heads that were placed at random across the wide-spreading grounds.

The ring of the telephone interrupted her reverie, and she hurried downstairs to answer it before it disturbed the sleeping stranger.

'Hi,' said Casey, 'everything OK? I wanted to call earlier, but I was sent out on an assignment.' He really loves that word, Lauren reflected with a smile. 'Has the man from nowhere been behaving himself?'

'He couldn't do otherwise,' Lauren pointed out. 'He's still weak from the illness he's had. Anyway—'

she frowned as her conscience pricked her '—last night I locked him in his room.'

There was a burst of laughter from the other end. 'Full marks to you, Lauren. What happened?'

'You mean, when he discovered it?' She could not tell him the whole truth. 'He roared like a caged lion. Well, you know what I mean. Anyway, he's in bed again.'

'How long's he staying?'

'I—' She hesitated, then decided to continue. 'I more or less told him to stay for as long as it takes him to recover.'

'You did?' Casey seemed a little shocked. 'How do you know you can trust him?'

I trust him, she thought, but did not know why. 'I just know I can,' was her deliberately evasive answer.

'Mmm, don't always trust your womanly intuition. What's his job, by the way?'

'I haven't discovered that much about him.'

'We—ell, I guess he could be unemployed. What's his name? Surely you know that.'

'It's Brett—Brett Carmichael.'

There was a sharp intake of breath, then, 'Hey, I've a hunch I've heard that name. Now...' He seemed to be finger-drumming, and she guessed he was at his office desk. 'This is going to be a tough one. First I'll ask around, then I'll look through back issues of newspapers—see if I can get a lead. Got to go, Lauren. I'll call you if I get any info on that name. Right?' He disconnected the call.

The sky was a clear blue, drawing Lauren into the garden with her sketchpad. She wandered round the flowerbeds, deciding which blooms to draw. A brilliantly red fuchsia caught her eye, and she squatted on her folding stool and assembled her crayons alongside the pad on the large drawing board she used for support.

Some time later a dragging sound caught her attention, and she turned to investigate. Brett was bumping a reclining garden chair and its extension across the lawn.

'Please carry on,' he said, unfolding it and arranging the sprung cushions, then attaching the footrest. 'I helped myself—' he indicated the chair '—hope you don't mind. I didn't want to disturb you.'

'Feel free,' Lauren commented airily. 'Maybe the fresh air will help you throw off your trouble. Better than lying in a stuffy room.'

'That's what I figured.'

He draped his length over the chair, arms folded, his legs stretching over the footrest. Lauren returned to her work, but the presence of the man seemed to have taken away her ability to concentrate. Nevertheless, she returned to her sketching, but, to her annoyance, the picture started to go wrong.

Something in her subconscious mind was troubling her, and it had something to do with the man beside her.

'That chair—where did you find it?'

'In the shed.'

The shed? She hadn't even noticed yet that there *was* a garden shed. And surely it was locked? Marie's uncle Redmund seemed to have a fixation about locking everything that could be opened.

'Where did you find the key?' she queried.

A shoulder lifted. 'In the kitchen, tucked away between the dresser and that ancient stove.'

'Truly? You went searching?' She smiled, but wondered if she should be worried instead. 'You must be good at tracking things down. Maybe you've got a sort of magnet in your head, and the metal key gave out a magnetic field?'

He gave a brief laugh, which made Lauren surmise that he was on the way to recovery. A small, irritating voice whispered, You don't want him to get better too soon, do you? She told it to be quiet.

'Maybe you're right,' he answered. There was a pause, then he said, 'Much of my life is spent in getting to the core of things.'

What do you do for a living? The thought formed in her mind but didn't make it to her lips. He was plainly a 'here today and gone tomorrow' kind of man, a wanderer. He had as good as told her that last night, and as a result he picked up things like fevers. So what he did for a living was none of her business, was it?

Strange, she pondered, remembering her conversation with Uncle Redmund that morning—he had been the second person she'd heard describe himself as a wanderer. But thousands of people wandered the world these days—young women, unattached men, as this man seemed to be.

'You make your living as an artist?' he queried, watching the movements of her hand but, low down as he was, unable to see what they were reproducing.

She nodded. 'Waiting for the next commission, wherever it might come from. Getting this job looking after Mr Gard's house was a great help in plugging the hole I would have made otherwise in my bank balance.' There was another pause, then, as her heartbeats revved to overdrive, she added as casually as she could, 'Did I give you a definite answer to your question about whether you can stay here? Anyway, the answer's yes.'

She glanced at him. Would he turn her down flat?

'Indefinitely?' An eyebrow lifted.

'If you like.'

'Thanks.'

It wasn't until she heard his answer, delivered in an equally casual tone, that her heart returned to its normal beat. Then a small, annoyingly sane voice asked, Have you done the right thing? How long will he stay? Can you *honestly* trust him? For heaven's sake, *who is he*?

For a while he seemed to be sleeping. As she worked Lauren tuned in to the sounds around her—the birdsong, a humming bee, a dog's distant bark, leaves moving in the breeze.

He stirred and stretched his long body, and Lauren's awareness of him immediately came to life. Why should her senses start reeling at the nearness of the man? OK, he was good-looking and clearly of high intelligence, with a magnetism about him that any woman would find difficult to resist.

So what? she tried telling herself. He was just another human being, wasn't he? No, he wasn't. She had to acknowledge that no other man had ever affected her in the way this stranger did.

She looked at him, and her pulses raced at the discovery that he had been watching her. He switched his attention to their surroundings.

'The quietness,' he commented, 'is so loud it almost deafens.'

'Do you prefer noise and bustle?'

'It's what I've had for months—years now.'

Every time he referred to his normal way of life— which just had to involve some occupation—it made her want to say, Tell me more about yourself. But once again she suppressed the urge.

It wasn't that she preferred him to be mysterious, she told herself, just that if—when—she did discover what he did for a living, it would—well, kind of break the spell.

Knowing so little about him—wasn't that part of the charm?—and liking him as she did, she felt it in her bones that if reality intruded it would bring an unwelcome end to the magic of the situation.

'You—you've left that behind, Mr Carmichael?' she ventured, then reproached herself for tempting that reality she dreaded into coming a little nearer. So she added quickly, 'What are you immediate aims?' That, she scolded herself, was also the wrong thing to say. Did she really want him to get up and go?

'The name's Brett,' he put in, adding with a quick smile, 'Lauren.'

She echoed that smile, nodding.

It took him a few moments to answer her question, then, rolling his head towards her and holding her gaze, he answered, 'I guess all I want at present is a bit of peace. Tranquillity of the soul.' He looked away, appearing to consider the words, as though they pleased him. His eyes sought hers again. 'I have this deep-down yearning for it. You know a place I could get that?'

His penetrating gaze seemed to be looking into *her* soul, and she caught her breath. Who was this stranger who had come into her life—disturbing her, agitating her more than any other man had ever done?

'Maybe. . .here?'

The words had slipped out, and once again she grew angry with herself for allowing them to do so.

His expression altered so subtly she thought she had imagined it, until his eyes, with a look that was entirely male, flickered over her. Then it was gone.

She shivered slightly, knowing that her suspicion that his normal masculine reflexes had merely been overlaid by his indisposition and not obliterated had been correct. When he transferred his gaze to their surroundings again, relief flooded through her.

'Thanks for the offer,' he responded casually, then stopped.

Was he going to turn it down? Her hand trembled just a little as she endeavoured unsuccessfully to continue with her sketching. Her heart began to sink, and angrily she told it that it was a fool to have got so involved. No, it answered back. It wasn't involvement, only sympathy and compassion. How could it be anything else?

He spoke again, startling her from her thoughts.

'You could be right, Lauren. Here I'll stay, until...
You agree?'

Until...? her mind echoed, and she wished he had not left the sentence unfinished.

'I agree, Brett.' That small voice added mischievously, And you never want him to go, do you? Never, she answered it. Never. Not even if he turns out to be the devil himself.

A few days later Lauren discovered Brett browsing in the library. It was a long room—probably formed, she estimated, when the cottages had been joined.

From ceiling to floor, its walls were lined with books. An ancient open fireplace, its stone hearth decorated with long grasses and artificial blooms, filled one end of the narrow room, while a writing desk and two upright chairs occupied the other.

It was in front of some shelves stacked with leatherbound, gold-embossed volumes that Brett stood, a book opened between his palms. He held it as if it were itself made of gold, almost as if it had some special meaning for him. But how could it? she argued. He was as new to this house as she was, and as unfamiliar with its contents.

She had entered quietly, and he only became aware of her presence when she turned to close the heavy wooden door. By the time she turned back he had replaced the volume and was inspecting the other shelves, his hands having found his pockets. Had he something to hide? The thought darted in and out of her mind.

A frisson of fear ran through her. Who *was* he? He might have been around the place for a few days now— though it seemed to her that it was more like two or three weeks, so accustomed had she grown to his being there—but she hadn't got to know him any better in that time.

He seemed to have taken on an air of remoteness, of holding himself apart. Was he, perhaps, going through a time of readjustment from whatever had plunged him into the low state in which he had picked up that fever?

She recalled his words: 'Tranquillity of the soul. I have this deep-down yearning for it.' The words still moved her deeply, and an overwhelming sense of empathy, of longing to comfort him, swept over her once again.

He had been friendly enough, she granted him that, and he had praised her cooking, joking about his own poor showing in that respect, but there was still this gulf between them, with not a bridge in sight to cross to the other side—to his side.

Now and then she had caught him watching her, but his expression had been so inscrutable she had been unable to decipher it. There had been more than a touch of male interest in it, which had caused her skin to prickle. There had been something else too, and it maddened her that yet again she was unable to read it.

'How high a star-rating would you give this library?' she asked, crossing the room. If she could join him before he moved, she calculated, she might just be able to pinpoint the book he had been reading with such concentration. It might give her a clue as to his occupation, that unknown side of him. 'Two stars? Three?'

It was too late. He had side-stepped some half a dozen paces before she could reach him.

'Five—no doubt about it,' he declared unequivocally.

'As good as that?' She continued with her smiling interrogation. 'What would you say was the owner's particular interest? Mr Gard's, I mean.'

'History.'

Lauren was a little taken aback by his lack of hesitation. 'How do you know?' she asked, and felt a little foolish when he glanced at her, eyebrows raised.

Had the lingering doubts—doubts more than sus-picion—that she still had of him shown?

'By deduction—how else?' was his faintly crushing reply, the sweep of his arm indicating the crowded bookshelves.

She nodded, crossing to read the titles opposite. 'Mr Gard must have wide interests. Plus a love of books, of course. But,' she wondered aloud, 'if he's the wanderer he claims to be, I don't know when he'd have the time to read them.'

'Agreed.' The word came succinctly from behind her. 'Lauren?'

A tingling shot up and down her spine at the sound of her name on his tongue. 'Mmm?'

She turned to find him at her shoulder, and the shock moved to sting that part of her anatomy. It worried her, this feeling she experienced whenever he was near. Hadn't Johnny, Casey's friend, warned her not to fall for him? A good-looking guy, he'd called Brett Carmichael that night, full of fever though the stranger had been. Johnny's warning had been so right, she realised now. But when had heart ever listened to intellect?

Her eyes sought his in question, and when his met hers there was a jolt inside her that almost knocked her off balance. It was his question, mundane as it was, that brought that balance back.

'I need some means of transport. Is there a car showroom in the village?'

He needed transport? He was leaving? She couldn't bear the thought. Nor could she ask him without giving herself away.

'There's the local garage. They sell secondhand vehi-cles. I have to go to the store this morning. I could give you a lift.'

He had moved, hands thrust into the pockets of his well-cut white casual trousers. His short-sleeved cotton shirt fitted well too, his tanned arms contrasting with its lemon colour. If he'd been living in the tropics, Lauren reflected, he would have needed light-coloured clothes for coolness, wouldn't he?

'OK, thanks.' He answered casually, almost dismissively, like a man who had vowed never again to allow emotion to govern his thoughts, his life.

He must have been badly hurt at some time, Lauren decided. And what else except by a woman? The idea of his ever having been so in love with a woman that she'd forced him to such a painful decision sent her heart into a dive, even as she tried to break its fall by berating it soundly.

The phone rang distantly and she excused herself, dashing out of the library and picking up the extension in the kitchen just in case it was Casey with news.

It was Casey. 'First, how are things?' he asked.

'OK. Fine. He needs a car.'

'Who doesn't? Did you tell him about the village garage?'

'I'm taking him there any minute. So what have you discovered?' She had lowered her voice, hooking the door closed with her foot.

'Not much. Nothing, in fact. I've asked around the local papers, and the not so local. One or two guys thought they'd heard the name, but couldn't remember in what connection.'

'He's coming, Casey. Must go. Keep trying, won't you?'

'Will do. Keep smiling. Keep your distance—or rather, make him keep his.'

'You've got to be joking,' was her laughing rejoinder. 'We might as well be on opposite sides of the globe.'

'Good. Keep it that way. I'll be in London for a couple of days,' he added hurriedly, before ending the call.

CHAPTER FOUR

LAUREN drove Brett to the car showroom, then, with a wave, drove off towards the village centre to visit the grocery store. Glancing back through her driving mirror, she saw him nosing round one of the cars as the salesman approached.

When she was paying for the goods at the checkout, the assistant, a local lady to whom she had introduced herself before, asked, 'How do you like living in Mr Gard's house?'

'Just fine, thanks.'

'We heard you had company.'

Oh, dear, village gossip, Lauren thought, collecting her change and loading the goods into her shopping bag.

'He's a paying guest,' she said, in what she hoped was a prim and proper tone as befitted a totally uninvolved landlady—which she was, wasn't she? 'He's very quiet.' You can say that again, she thought. 'And is recovering very well from an illness he had when he arrived.'

'Oh, good,' the assistant returned with a smile. No suspicion there of any moral wrong-doing on anyone's part, Lauren decided. Thank goodness. And nor was there any, she thought, leaving the store and stacking the shopping in her car.

As she drove back past the garage she looked for Brett, but there was no sign. Her heart nearly stopped when she did see him. He was lounging, hands in pockets, against the bus stop sign. A bus was due, she knew that, but what was he doing going into the town?

* * *

Three hours later, a long, low, *brand-new* car drew up in the drive. Mouth open on a gasp, Lauren, from her workroom upstairs, watched her paying guest emerge from the driving seat and slam the door, turning to admire his purchase.

She was overcome by an acute fear that this was the outside world putting its harsh foot in the door just before bursting in to destroy the fragile togetherness that had been forming between them.

Withdrawing from her position at the window, she returned to the task of arranging her watercolours, hanging on convenient picture hooks those already framed.

As swift footsteps took the stairs she stood back, heartbeats racing, pretending to admire her own handiwork. The door swung open and Brett stood there, a light in his eyes.

'You've seen my new possession?'

She nodded. 'Oh, wow,' she said, her voice coming out low-key in spite of her doing her best to sound as excited as he was. 'It's great. But—? Oh, of course—you've got it on hire.'

'Nope. It's mine. It's OK—' he smiled at her bewilderment '—I didn't have to rob a bank to buy it.'

Which surely meant that he might be a stranger come in from the cold—or rather, the heat, judging by his tan—but he certainly wasn't poverty-stricken.

He walked to the window and stared down at his car, then restlessly wandered about, studying the paintings and sketches which Lauren had arranged round the room.

'Are all these works yours?'

'They are.'

There was silence while she held her breath for his comments. He moved from one to the other and her heart sank. He's going to be kind, she thought. Say something like 'just great' without meaning it, then go back to drooling over his new possession.

Still he said nothing, and she couldn't bear it. 'So I know they're mediocre and I've got no real talent,' she burst out, 'which is probably why I haven't got a job at the moment. You can stop pretending you're interested in them. . .'

He had turned, eyebrows arching over a strange light in his eyes. 'You're uttering garbage, Lauren, and you know it.' He strolled to stand in front of her. 'Stop talking yourself down. You're good.'

Her throat went dry at the gleam in his eyes, the curve of his expressive mouth.

Her heart beat like a drum. 'You. . .you're experienced in these matters? You can tell gold from dross?'

His hands lifted, cupping her cheeks. 'Oh, yes,' he said softly, 'I know pure gold when I see it.'

His mouth lowered, touching hers. Lifting his head, he looked into her eyes. The drumroll in her chest was almost shaking her. What could he read in her gaze? She didn't know, nor did she care. She *wanted* those lips on hers. She'd wanted them there, hadn't she, ever since she'd first set eyes on him?

'Not a no in sight,' he commented huskily. He loosened his hold. 'Not a single shake of the head.' His hands imprisoned her face again, but more tightly now, so that she couldn't have evaded those lowering lips even if she had wanted to.

Brett took his kiss lightly, then with a pressure that began a meltdown of any resistance inside her that might have managed to survive in the face of that purposeful mouth. Then the invasion began, first forcing open her lips, then intruding, finding her tongue, straying to discover the hollows and caverns within.

His arms fastened round her and she melted entirely, her legs forgetting their true function of supporting her, forcing her to lift her arms and wrap them around his neck. Oh, God, she thought, he'll think I'm an easy target, willing to let any man take me. . .

'Brett,' she managed, as for a second he freed her mouth, 'please. . .I'm not—'

'Oh, but you are,' he breathed against her lips. 'You're dynamite, Miss Halstead. I've been wanting this since the moment we met. And don't deny that you've wanted it too.'

His eyes held hers and she saw the light in them. Then it came to her why he was in this mood. It was not she, Lauren Halstead, who had aroused his passion. He was on a high, wasn't he, having acquired an expensive toy? That gleaming new car that stood outside.

Wheels skidding on gravel brought her back to earth. His hands slid into his pockets and he watched as she patted her flushed cheeks and attempted to tidy her hair. He smiled, saying nothing.

A hammering at the door followed by a shout told them both that Lauren had company, also that company's identity. Brett's smile faded. Lauren's heart sank into its rightful place. She scuttled down the stairs, calling, 'OK, Casey. I'm on my way.'

Casey's eyes were alight, too, but plainly for a very different reason. Still on the doorstep, he glanced around. 'Where's the lodger?'

'Upstairs. Why?'

Looking behind him furtively, he beckoned her round the corner and into the rear gardens.

'I've got news.'

'About—Brett Carmichael?' She was filled with foreboding. She wanted him—willed him—to say no. She had the terrible feeling that the information Casey was bursting to give her would shatter the tenuous relationship that had formed between herself and the stranger, would draw a cancelling line through whatever might have been starting between them.

'About Brett Carmichael—who else? Know what his line is? He's— No, wait a minute. I've got no assignments this evening.' His glance was calculating. 'Doing anything tonight?'

'Washing my hair.'

'So what's new?' he commented disbelievingly.

A car door slammed, an engine roared and wheels crackled on the driveway. Brett had gone out. Well, he has every right to, hasn't he? Lauren scolded her drooping spirits which, since his kisses, had been floating on a cloud.

'Do your hair-washing tomorrow and have dinner with me tonight,' Casey pressed. 'Then I'll tell you more.'

'That's blackmail,' Lauren protested.

Casey grinned. 'Personally, I'd call it *white*mail. You get something out of it, and so do I—your company.'

He held all the cards and Lauren knew it. If she wanted to know more about Brett Carmichael—which, against her better judgement, she did—she'd have to agree.

She sighed and smiled at the same time. 'What time?'

'I'll call for you—say, seven?'

'Seven,' Lauren agreed, and waved him on his way.

'He's a journalist,' Casey told her over their aperitifs. 'Hadn't you guessed?'

The hotel dining room was crowded, the chatter of the guests causing Casey to move nearer.

'A *journalist*?'

'Dictionaries and I,' he'd said, 'are on very familiar terms.' And hadn't he appreciated the word 'quasi', which she'd used to describe Marie's uncle Redmund? Of course she should have guessed, she reproached herself.

'Yep, the same line as me,' Casey was saying. 'I've been in London for a couple of days, so I asked around. Struck gold through one of the national dailies—a contact I have there.'

'And?'

'And. . .no wonder he can afford that macho means of transport I saw lined up in your driveway. For some years, my contact said, he owned his own news agency down under, gathering and sending out news from around the globe.'

'Which is maybe why we didn't recognise his name. Although you thought you'd heard of him, didn't you?'

He nodded. 'A year or so ago, apparently, he sold the agency and went on a world walkabout, working freelance for his old firm.' Casey counted on his fingers. 'South America, the Far East, the jungles of Africa.'

'And that's how he picked up that fever?'

Casey lifted his shoulders. 'And get this—he's been captured and held hostage by rebels, or some such in some country or other.'

Lauren shuddered, not even daring to think about the terrible things that could have happened to him during his imprisonment. Then she remembered with horror how that first night she had locked him in, *imprisoned* him in his room. No wonder he had got so mad with her. 'Never,' he'd said, 'never do that to me again.' Now she knew why!

'Over there—' Casey leaned nearer, voice lowered '—is my editor. He's eyeing you, Lauren. Bet he tackles me tomorrow, asks who my new girlfriend is.' Now he eyed her himself, up and down. 'Likes what he sees, obviously.' Casey's grin was wide. 'I like what I see too. White top, nice fit, shows off your—' his gaze dropped a little '—er—shape. Suits your colouring too. Sets off your chestnut hair—isn't that what they call browny-red?'

'Stop it, will you?' Lauren urged, turning pink.

'Not to mention your dreamy eyes. A guy could get lost in them. And that mouth—perfect shape, just like the rest of—'

'You've slipped into repeat mode, Casey,' Lauren hissed. 'Press the "off" button, will you? Or I'll. . .'

'OK, I will—for now. But I bet when I tell Harry Harper who I've discovered living among us—'

'You mean Brett Carmichael?' Lauren cut in sharply, anxiously. 'For heaven's sake, Casey, don't—please don't breathe a word to him about Brett.'

'Hey, you're asking me to put my scoop under wraps? I've got ambition, Lauren.'

'Where's the scoop in printing stuff about a man like Brett? He's been in the southern hemisphere for years, according to you.'

Casey shrugged, plainly capitulating, but reluctantly. 'So I'll bide my time. Maybe I'll find out more some day. Anyway...' Casey tucked into his meal in earnest now, and gestured to Lauren to do the same. 'The mystery is, why has he come back now to his native soil?'

Lauren frowned, thoughtfully chewing a forkful of herb-flavoured casseroled chicken. 'And why did he find his way to Old Cedar Grange?'

'Ask the guy—why not?'

'Oh, no. Not my business. Nor is it my house.'

'So,' he said, with an 'I've got you' smile, 'wasn't it just a bit checky of you to accept him into it as a paying guest without getting permission first?'

'What else could I do? He was ill; you know that. I couldn't turn him away. Mr Gard can't be contacted except in a dire emergency and Marie's disappeared into the blue with her Reggie. Anyway, he's paying good money—and to the owner, not to me. I'm sure Mr Gard wouldn't object. And at least it means I'm not alone.'

'Hey—' Casey put his hand over Lauren's '—I'd have kept you company. One little crook of your finger and I'd have swapped my rotten lodgings for a room there.'

Lauren felt a little awkward at Casey's declaration. 'Thanks for the compliment, but... Anyway, I'd have

thought it obvious why he came back. His illness—
homing instinct after his awful experiences.'

Suddenly something drew her eyes, and her heart
nearly stopped. Across the room, Brett sat back in his
chair, aperitif at the ready, eyes on them. Removing
her hand from under Casey's, she kept her knowledge
of Brett's presence to herself. If she revealed so much
as the slightest awareness of him, Casey would be over
there in two seconds and introducing him to his editor.

To her relief, the rest of the meal passed without
incident—except that through her side vision she saw
Brett leave the restaurant without a single glance in
their direction.

Later, standing in the doorway of Old Cedar Grange,
Casey held her shoulders, smiling down at her. 'If any
more info comes my way reference you-know-who, I'll
get in touch.' His mouth found hers and took a soft,
lingering kiss. 'Mmm, they taste as good as they look.
Thanks for your company.'

She hadn't had time to object, but even if she had,
she thought, she wouldn't have done. He'd bought her
a meal, hadn't he?

A car approached, its headlights sweeping the house
and their figures close together, then braked.

'Oh-oh, here comes trouble.' Casey removed his
arms from around her back.

'Please, Casey,' Lauren whispered, catching at one
of his jacket lapels, 'don't say a word to your editor
about him.'

'We—ell. . .' He pretended to consider her plea.
'Give me another kiss and maybe I won't.'

She let him take the quick kiss he had asked for.

'See you,' he called, opening his car door. Moments
later, the wheels spurted gravel and he sped past Brett
as he locked his own car.

Lauren moved from the doorway, allowing Brett to
pass, then made for the kitchen. When he grabbed her
arm and swung her round she could not suppress a

gasp as she overbalanced and fell against him. Annoyance fought with the pleasure she experienced at the renewed contact with his body, heating her cheeks.

'What have I d-done to d-deserve that?' The words came jerkily from her.

'Your Romeo, otherwise known as our tame neighbourhood sleuth, has enlightened you as to my occupation, has he? Over the meal you shared with him?'

His leg and thigh were in close contact with hers, which flustered her still further. She found herself wanting even closer contact. . .

'How did you know *he* was a journalist too?' she prevaricated, wishing she had been able to control the waver in her tone.

'It takes a member of the rat-pack to know another. I could see it in his eyes, his movements, his manner. I even managed to tune in to his thought-processes. So now you know what you've been itching to know from the moment we met.'

Her head snapped back and she managed somehow to put a distance between them. 'It's only natural, isn't it, for a—a landlady to know something about her tenant's background? You came out of the blue, in the dark, round the back of the house. Like a—like a—'

'Thief in the night. OK, I get you.' He turned away, scanning the gardens in the fading light, his gaze coming to rest on the giant cedar tree against which he had slumped with weakness on the evening of his arrival.

'Brett?'

He turned back slowly.

'I didn't know you'd been held hostage.'

His eyebrows lifted slowly. 'So?'

'I—I'm sorry—truly sorry for locking you in that first night. It—it must have brought back some dreadful memories.'

He walked on into the kitchen, taking the kettle,

running water into it and switching it on. Lauren
followed him, watching his movements.

'Are they too painful to talk about?' she pressed,
then chided herself for psychologically mishandling
him. If he wanted to talk about it, he would, wouldn't
he? In his own good time?

'Coffee?' was his only response.

And when she said, 'Please,' he filled two mugs and
handed her one.

He took a mouthful and made his way past her into
the living room. He did not take a seat but wandered
to the window, staring out, drinking.

Lauren sat on one of the three-seater sofas, sipping
her coffee and feeling tiredness wash over her. Keeping
Casey company had been something of a strain. Had it
been because she'd been aware for much of the time of
Brett's watching, plainly disapproving presence across
the restaurant.

'Is Talbert your boyfriend?'

At first Lauren was puzzled. 'Talbert?' Then she
realised to whom he was referring. 'Oh, you mean
Casey. No, just a friend. I didn't know of his existence
until Marie's party—the night you arrived. Inciden-
tally—' she frowned '—how did you know his
surname?'

'I rang the local newspaper. They told me, yes, a
man called Casey was a staff reporter. Then I asked for
his full name, which they gave me.'

Of course. Being a member of the journalistic profession, he knew the ropes where obtaining information
was concerned.

Brett half turned. 'And you're already on kissing and
dating terms?'

'I only met you that same night, yet we—you and I—
have kissed.' As soon as she had spoken she wished the
floor would open up. She'd asked for his scorn, which
duly came her way.

'True,' he drawled, turning fully now and raking her

with a cynical gaze. 'So you're in the habit of kissing—
and God knows what else—any man, however short
your acquaintance with him?' He finished his coffee,
putting his mug aside.

'The answer's no, but I don't suppose you'll believe
me. Casey had bought me a meal—'

'And he'd given you information about me,' he
continued tauntingly. 'Which naturally merited a vote
of thanks on your part, which, from the look of it, took
the form of a petting session.'

Lauren lifted her shoulders, curiously wanting to cry.
She knew he had been deliberately insulting, but she
couldn't tell him, could she, that she infinitely preferred
his kisses to Casey's? That Casey's kisses hadn't
touched her, whereas his, Brett's, had sent her heart
into a spin and almost turned her legs to the consistency
of melting snow.

Instead, she drained her mug and went to collect his,
hiding her trembling lip by going into the kitchen. He
caught up with her as she slammed the door of the
dishwasher. She tried to slip past him but he turned her
by the shoulders, watching the tremulous movement of
her lips. Slowly he lowered his mouth, touching down
on hers and stilling the movement.

He lifted his head, staring at her brimming eyes. 'Tell
me why.'

'Why, what?' she asked thickly.

'Why the tears.' With his forefinger he lifted a
teardrop and studied it as if it were a crystal ball. 'It's
not divulging its secrets,' he commented with a smile.
'So. . .?'

'You're—you're so good at saying the wrong thing,'
she blurted out, wiping her cheeks with the back of her
hand. 'Not to mention believing the worst of anybody.'

'So there's nothing between you and that guy?'

'There's no reason why I should reply to that question, but the answer's no.'

For a long moment he stared at her lips, and her

heart beat even faster at the thought that his mouth was about to take over hers again. But his hands dropped away and she had to quell a flash of disappointment.

He wandered back to the living room, Lauren following him to collect the jacket she had dropped onto a chair.

'Lauren?'

'Yes?' She paused on her way to the door, unable to deny the spurt of pleasure she felt at the way he'd spoken her name. 'In the next few months I'll be working on a book.'

Next few months? He was intending to stay that long? It was necessary to quell yet another spurt of pleasure.

'You will? Will it be about your experiences?'

'What experiences?' His voice had a hard edge.

She stayed silent and still, keeping her body language, she hoped, to the minimum. But he read the message in her lack of response.

His eyes narrowed. 'I must ask you to promise me something, otherwise I shall have to pack my bags and move on.'

'You—you mean, leave here?' This time the dismay in her voice, let alone the language of her body, let her down.

'Exactly that. Which would deprive me of the kind of sanctuary I'm beginning to believe I might have found here—temporary though it may be—and you of the rent I pay.'

'The owner,' she corrected automatically.

His shoulders lifted. 'Whatever.' He approached slowly. 'Will you promise, hand on heart, to divulge nothing—*nothing*—about me, my thoughts, my movements, to your reporter friend?'

'Do you really think I'd act as a *spy* where you're concerned? What do you think I am—a sneak?'

'It's surprising what some people will do for money.'

'Well, Mr Carmichael, exclude me from your sweeping statement,' she threw back at him, head high. 'I'm on the level.' Her anger almost shook her. 'So level that on a clear day you can see my character for miles.'

There was a long pause while he studied her face, finishing with her eyes. They had taken on an uncertain expression, and his softened strangely.

'Hand on heart.' She put her hand beneath her left breast. 'I promise. Now do you believe me?'

'OK, Miss Halstead, I believe you.' Then he smiled. 'You have an intriguing way with words.' Reaching out, he placed his hand over hers, brushing against her breast, causing her heartbeats to double their speed.

Then he moved her hand, pulling her towards him. 'Shall we seal our bargain?'

He took her jacket from her and threw it back onto the chair. When his mouth descended she took no steps to evade it. Her lips quivered as his made contact, and when his arms moved to gather her into them she could find no objection within herself to the feel of his hard body against the yielding softness of hers.

That kiss was followed by another, after which he continued to hold her, his cheek on her hair, her face against his chest. She revelled in the sensation of being where she was, inhaling his own special scent, wanting to slip her hand inside his shirt to feel his bone structure, his muscled leanness. Through the fine fabric of his shirt she could detect the roughness of his chest hair.

He made no sound nor movement. He just stood holding her, his breath stirring tendrils of her hair, fanning her neck, bringing a tingling to her sensitised skin and an enveloping warmth to her heart.

It was almost as if he could not tear himself away, as if he needed her in his arms—needed any woman, she deliberately rationalised, in an attempt to bring herself down to earth—to erase the awful memories that would not let him be.

He released her at last, standing back, hands in pockets. A coldness swirled around Lauren as if she had stepped into winter air from the warmth of a summer's day.

'Good—' She had to clear her throat. 'Goodnight, Brett.'

He inclined his head, lips curved, eyes seemingly reminiscent of the kisses they had just shared.

CHAPTER FIVE

THE sun illuminated the world outside, warming the air and bringing a glow to the blossoming flowers. It was too nice a day, Lauren decided, to spend working indoors.

She gathered some sheets of cartridge paper into a folder and piled chalks and crayons into a flat box, all of which she pushed into a large bag which she swung onto her shoulder, holding her small folding stool in one hand and a backing board in her other.

There had been no sign or sound of Brett, and when he started descending the stairs she was startled into staring up at him.

He smiled. 'You look as if you've seen a ghost,' he remarked lightly.

She had! 'A very substantial ghost,' she joked, to hide her puzzlement. Once again she felt she had seen his face before—yet where, she could not for the life of her pinpoint.

'Where are you off to? Or shouldn't I ask?'

'Not to an assignation, if that's what you're thinking.'

He was level with her now, and held up his hand as if shielding himself from her indignation. 'OK, a shot across my bows. I'll stage a retreat and get myself some breakfast.'

'Please help yourself. You know where everything is by now.' Opening the front door, she relented. 'I'm going to a place called Millstream Valley. It's owned by the National Trust and its scenery is fantastic. Being a stranger to these parts, you wouldn't have heard of it. It's tucked away, and unless you know where it is you could easily drive past it. Bye. Enjoy your peace and quiet.'

'Oh, I will, lady.' He smiled back at her.

It took her twenty minutes to reach Millstream Valley, after driving through the town and turning off the main road. She halted at the warden's box and showed her Trust membership card, at which he waved her on, saluting in recognition. Some way into the valley, she parked the car and extracted her sketching equipment, including the small stool.

As she always did when visiting the area, she stood for a few minutes just taking in the beauty of the place. The hills rose fantastically each side of the valley and the stream wound its way through the gorge, crossed here and there by wooden bridges.

After walking to the water's edge, she set up her stool and board with the sketching paper covering it, placing her materials beside her on the grass. She did not intend to restrict her work that morning to drawing wild flowers. Instead, having selected the appropriate crayons, she began to draw with a sweeping hand the hillside facing her.

So absorbed was she that she scarcely noted the crunch on gravel of a vehicle's wheels, and only glanced up when a car boot slammed and footsteps approached.

A gasp caught at her throat as she identified the newcomer. 'How did you manage to find this place?' she asked Brett as he came to stand beside her.

'Maps have been invented,' he remarked laconically, which was all the explanation Lauren guessed would come her way. But of course; she had given him the name of the place, hadn't she? All the same, even with a map, it was no easy place to find.

'May I?' He dropped beside her onto the grass.

Without turning her head, Lauren sensed him looking around.

'Isn't it as fantastic as I said it was?' she asked, feeling her senses heightened by his presence. The grass had become curiously greener, the sun more brilliant, the sky a more intense blue.

He inhaled deeply, and slowly let out the breath. 'Words can hardly do it justice,' was his considered comment.

'Is this a place where you could find that tranquillity of soul you said you were looking for?'

There was a long pause before he answered, then, with a prolonged gaze around, ending with a glance in her direction, he said, 'Maybe.'

He lay back full length, hands supporting his head, and Lauren's senses became agitated. Before her eyes the colours around her changed and deepened, dancing madly, taking on each other's shades, confusing her entirely. This is useless, she thought. I'll have to wait until things become normal again.

'Why have you stopped working?'

The question agitated her still more, making her look at the reclining figure, and her artist's mind began to analyse his long, solid frame. This was quickly over-taken by her feminine reflexes as they made her wonder what it would be like to lie with him, come under his domination, make love with him. . .

'I haven't stopped,' she stated firmly, but knew that it wasn't coming right, that her emotions had intruded on her objective approach and ruined her efforts.

With a short, irritated breath, she put the drawing aside and clasped her arms round her bent knees. There was silence between them for a few minutes—a silence deeper than that around them.

When her arm was caught by strong fingers and she was pulled sideways, so that she rolled against him, she started to fight him—to press her bent knees into his stomach, to pummel his chest.

Clearly aroused, but not in the least pained by her belligerent actions, he pushed her onto her back, pressing at her legs until they unbent. He rolled onto her, catching her chin and placing his mouth on hers. It was not a gentle kiss, but hard and intrusive, demanding a response which Lauren tried to suppress but found that she was quite unable to.

Her arms lifted and curved around his neck, thus offering up her entire self to his demands. His hand tunnelled under her cotton top, found a breast covered by lace, jerked aside the lace and cupped that breast with a wide, moulding palm.

'Brett?'

Still holding her breast, he released her mouth, both of which continued to throb from his potent arousal of them. He gazed down at her flushed face, riveting his eyes on hers. 'A guy,' Mitch had once said, 'could lose himself in those eyes of yours.' Was that what Brett was doing, losing himself, his bad memories, in her eyes?

Was his lovemaking a form of escape too, helping him forget the past, maybe even a woman he had loved and lost? One thing she knew she could be sure of, Lauren told herself sadly, was that his kissing and his sudden possessiveness of her body didn't arise from any deep feeling for her—how could it after such a short acquaintance?—but from what must have been a long period of abstinence, of a total absence of female company.

'Yes?' he answered at last.

'Why?'

'Why not?' was his succint, if totally unsatisfactory reply.

Slowly he released her breast, sliding his hand from under her top and allowing her to wriggle from under him—which action, she discovered to her dismay, aroused her longings for him even more.

He reclined on his elbow, watching as she tried to smooth her hair and put her clothes to rights.

'You've totally upset my concentration,' she told him, infusing a petulance into her voice which she did not feel.

'So take a break and we'll go and find a place where

we can get lunch. Further along the valley there's a teashop. Yes?'

With a resigned sigh at having to abandon her work, she gathered her belongings and nodded. What could be better than finding Brett Carmichael across the table and sharing a meal with him?

It did cross her mind to wonder how he knew the teashop, but she decided that he must have driven a short distance along the valley looking for her, before turning round and coming back, finally discovering where she was working.

They sat side by side at a table, Lauren choosing Stilton and broccoli soup and salmon sandwiches, while Brett opted for vegetable pasta and a side salad. As they ate Brett gazed thoughtfully out at the dramatic rise of the hillside across the stream, saying little, while Lauren found pleasure in just sitting beside him. He was close enough for her to feel the slight pressure of his thigh against hers, and she was quite unable to quell the wanton sensations that invaded her and threatened to inflame yet again her feminine desires.

Brett fetched coffee, and as he drank she glanced at him, finding a smile in his eyes which were turned towards her.

'What have you been thinking?' he asked, leaning back and placing his arm behind her along the back of the bench seat they shared.

She smiled up at him. 'Wondering what *you* were thinking.'

His smile faded and he lifted his shoulders.

'Were you remembering the. . .' dared she? she wondered '. . .the things that happened to you?'

'Maybe.'

There was an uncertain pause, then she ventured, 'Were they too terrible for you to speak about?'

Another pause, from him this time. 'They weren't

pleasant. Looking out there. . .at the peace it holds, the quiet beauty—'

'When all the time in your head you hear gunfire and threats and cries?' A sharp movement from him silenced her momentarily, but she ventured, 'How was it they freed you?'

He shrugged. 'After a while they got fed up with me, let me go.'

Lauren's eyes fluttered closed in sheer relief.

A car swung into the car park opposite, and an 'Oh, no' erupted into Lauren's mind.

Spying them through the window, Casey Talbert waved, then strode across and entered the café.

'May I?' Without waiting for an answer, he seated himself across from them. He saw their empty dishes. 'You've eaten? I'm famished.'

To Lauren's dismay, Brett rose and made to go.

'Don't let me disturb you,' Casey said, on his way to the counter. 'Carry on—finish your lunch.'

'I've had sufficient,' Brett replied, adding a reluctant, 'Thanks.' He nodded to Lauren, making for the door.

Wasn't there anything she could do or say, she thought, racking her brains, to prevent him from leaving?

'I hope you enjoyed your—your peace and quiet,' were the first words that sprang to mind.

He half turned, his smile brittle, his eyes reminiscent. 'Thank you, yes. I enjoyed my *peace and quiet* very much.'

Casey glanced at Brett as he carried his coffee and plate of sandwiches across, then at Lauren, seeing her rising colour. 'What's going on, Lauren?'

She pretended innocence, shaking her head.

'Between you two,' Casey added.

'Nothing,' she snapped. 'How did you know I was here?'

'Just happened to look out of the office window a couple of hours ago and saw you drive past. The turning for the valley is almost opposite our car park. Right? I guessed you were going sketching. Right again?'

'I forgot what an inspired news-gatherer you were,' Lauren commented sourly.

'Yep.' He had taken her sarcastic remark as a compliment. 'Nothing much passes Casey Talbert's radar detection equipment.' He tapped his eyes, ears and head.

'You've got a very high opinion of yourself.'

He affected a deep, astonished frown. 'I *have*? Anyway, you haven't asked me why I chased you all this way.'

'So why?'

His grin became sheepish. 'To spend half an hour in your company. You get to a guy, Lauren.'

She watched Casey chewing his way through his lunch. 'You must have been hungry.'

'Yeah, for you.' He grinned again.

'Drop the very *un*seductive clichés, *please*,' she begged.

'Sorry.' He wrote with his forefinger on an invisible blackboard. 'Must learn to be more subtle. Er—what's your line? Do you realise I've never asked?'

Instead of answering she took her portfolio from the floor beside her and, pushing away the used crockery, made a space for it on the table.

Casey's eyes opened wide. 'You're an artist? Hey,' he exclaimed as she took out that morning's work, 'they're good.'

Lauren, however, saw the faults, knowing that they were not her best work. There, she thought, looking at a mistake in her shading in of the hillside, is where Brett joined me. Here's where he looked at me in a certain way. And that squiggle is where I wondered what making love with him would be like. . .

'Ever exhibited your work?' Casey was asking eagerly. 'No? Well, I've got an uncle who owns a restaurant just outside town and he has a spare room upstairs. He might be willing to let you have it for an exhibition. Like the idea?'

'We-ell—' she put away her drawings '—it would be a great outlet, but—' She sighed. 'Who'd want to—?'

'Look at it? You'd have a ready-made audience, Lauren—all those wealthy dinner guests with money for luxuries. They'd have to be loaded to eat at my uncle's place. High-class stuff. How about...?' He looked at the wall-clock. 'I've got an hour before my appointment to interview a local councillor. How about me taking you there now?'

He swallowed his coffee and pushed back his chair. 'I'll go first,' he called over his shoulder as they crossed the narrow road to the car park, 'and you tail me in your car.'

Twenty minutes later, Lauren followed Casey into the circular drive of a large Victorian house. Above the main entrance door were the words 'Chez Talbert'.

Casey's uncle, rotund and beaming, was delighted with the pictures which Lauren set out on his office desk.

'The room is yours whenever you feel ready for it,' he told Lauren. 'Casey, take your friend upstairs and show her the gallery.'

'It's just great, Mr Talbert,' Lauren declared as she came down again some time later, Casey behind her. 'It'll be a chance to sell some of my stuff. I've never done it before. You'll want a commission, I quite understand that.'

Casey's uncle Henry frowned. 'Not one cent, my dear. It will be a great opportunity for you to get your name known and, I have to admit, also my restaurant's! And you've got my nephew here ready and waiting, haven't you, to give you a write-up in his paper?'

'Yeah, that's a great idea, Uncle.' Casey consulted his watch. 'Have to go. See you soon, Lauren, and we'll get on with arranging the necessary hype.'

Driving home, Lauren could hardly believe her luck. She approached Old Cedar Grange and swung the car to a standstill in front of the house. Then her spirits took a dive. Brett's car was missing from the driveway. Ridiculous thoughts tumbled around in her head.

He'd lost his way returning from Millstream Valley... He'd gone on a long drive without telling her... He'd packed his bags and left without a word...

Scrambling from the car, she raced to the entrance door and inserted her key. From the side of the house there came a series of thumps. Holding her breath, she withdrew her key and crept along to the closed garage doors.

A repeat of the sounds had her pulling at the door lever. As it swung up and over she jumped with fright. Then her spirits sprouted wings again, soaring. In front of her gleamed Brett's scarlet, low-slung four-wheeled pride and joy, and through the rear door she glimpsed a man moving about—a man she was coming to know more and more with every passing day.

'What are you doing?' she called, easing round the car. 'And how did you get in here?'

The sight of Brett stripped to the waist almost took her breath away. It was true that she had seen him before bare-chested, but then he had been weak and feverish. Now his masculinity sprang at her, overpowering her senses and making her want to rush into his arms...

'To answer your first question—' he looked around at the objects that were strewn over the concrete path '—I'm clearing out the rubbish. And I got in by using the key.'

'But...' She frowned. 'I've scoured the place for it.'

He shrugged his broad bare shoulders. 'I found it in a kitchen drawer. Right at the back,' he added. 'Which is where—' He broke off, then continued, 'Which is where everything anyone is looking for is usually found.'

'What are those pieces of wood in your hand?'

'What's this—an interrogation?' He seemed faintly annoyed. 'The next time you put your landlady's hat on, give me warning, will you?'

'I'm sorry, but I'm responsible for this residence, and I'm—'

'Only doing your duty. And you want to know what these are? This appears to be a matchbox-holder.' He discarded it and held up another item. 'A kind of fruit dish? Pretty crude. And this—' He paused, a frown pleating his forehead. 'Probably some schoolboy's very amateurish efforts at carpentry.' Beside him on the ground were two or three other roughly carved items.

'What are you going to do with them?' she asked.

'Junk the lot. What else?'

'Brett, you can't do that. They belong to the owner, Mr Gard.'

'They do?' Again his shoulders lifted and fell. 'So,' he drawled as if the subject bored him, 'you'll salvage them, will you?' He smiled. 'If I ask you nicely?'

She laughed. Did he know the effect he had on a woman when his mouth curved, his eyes lit up? When his tanned torso gleamed in the sunshine, the spread of chest hair inviting a feminine cheek to rub against it. . .?

Gathering up the wooden items, she dropped them into the bag he offered her.

'Brett, I must tell you,' she said. 'Casey Talbert—'

He visibly stiffened at the name.

'Casey's uncle has offered me a room so that I can stage an exhibition of my work.'

Brett seized a broom and swept some rubbish into a plastic bag.

'Aren't you pleased? For my sake?' she asked, her pleasure dimmed by his apparent lack of interest.

'Of course.' His voice was flat.

Well, why should he be pleased for her? she asked herself, turning away and dumping the schoolboy artefacts on the doorstep, then retrieving her sketches from the car.

He is only a tenant, she reminded herself firmly, and I'm simply his landlady. But did tenants usually kiss their landladies as he had kissed her? Did they begin to make love to them as he had to her?

He was like a jigsaw, she decided. There were so many parts to him that it was impossible to make a whole picture of his true self because there were so many pieces missing.

'Lauren.'

He had followed her into the house, pulling on a T-shirt and tucking it into his jeans. He pocketed his hands and waited until she had dumped the bag with its contents on the kitchen floor and deposited her belongings on the wooden table.

'Yes?' She looked at him, finding his cool gaze on her.

He was his aloof self again, wrapped around in his old remoteness. Kisses or no kisses, she thought sadly, would she—would any woman—ever totally break down the barrier—mental, not physical—that he perpetually seemed to erect between himself and the rest of man—and woman— kind?

She tried to smile but failed, realising with a shock just what was happening to her, and it frightened her to her core. She was falling for this man she had taken into the house. Against all the dictates of her common sense she was beginning to allow him to mean more to her than any other man she had ever known.

'With your permission,' he was saying, 'I'm going to purchase a computer.'

'My permission?'

'As my landlady.'

She'd almost forgotten her role! But was it any wonder? she asked herself. He'd settled in so well it was as if he actually belonged—to the house, in her life. No, that must not be, she told herself. Brett

Carmichael, truly male, just *had* to have a woman already in his life—a serious woman, not merely a passing stranger, as she was to him.

'Of course you have my permission,' she answered. 'Why ever not?'

She did not see him until next morning, and even then she heard him first.

Tracing the clatter to the kitchen, she stared at the man who sat at an ancient portable typewriter, thumping the keys adroitly with his forefingers as if he had done the same thing many times.

'Where did you unearth that object from?' she asked, hardly able to believe her eyes.

He smiled faintly at the words on the paper in the machine. 'I found it at the back of a cupboard.'

At the back of a drawer—at the back of a cupboard... How many more things was he going to discover hidden away?

He looked at her. 'You think your tenant—?'

'Mr Gard's tenant,' she corrected automatically.

'Your tenant,' he repeated, as if she had not spoken, 'is overstepping the mark? You think he's snooping around the place with doubtful intentions?'

'Yes.' It came out unequivocally.

He laughed, head back, and her heart did a jig at the sound, at the way it eased the tension from his face—a hangover, no doubt, from his past ordeals at the hands of his abductors.

He scraped back his chair and stood in front of her, tipping back her head with the long fingers of one hand, his other smoothing her hair from her forehead. It was as if they were lovers, accustomed to being close, being drawn to each other whenever they were in the same room, eager to breathe the same air.

When his arms went round her she did not resist. When his lips lowered to touch hers she let hers move beneath his mouth, accepting the kiss, giving it back...

He lifted his head, smiling down at her, then lowered his mouth again, as if hers held a magnet which he found irresistible.

But they weren't lovers. Touching and exchanging kisses didn't make them so. Which meant that she, Lauren, should put up the barriers which at that moment—because he desired the taste and feel of a woman in his arms—he had dismantled.

Except that he still kept the essence of him strictly to himself. She no more knew the true character of him now than when he had first emerged that night from the darkness into the lights of the house. In that respect he was still a stranger.

'Brett—'

He let her go, no doubt having heard the note of strain in her voice. Staring down at the words on the paper, he said, 'I decided to use this because I was already writing my book in my head. I reckoned that any old thing would do to record it on.'

'So as usual you went snooping in all the hidden corners.'

He lifted a shoulder. 'You were out so I couldn't ask your permission to—'

'Ransack the place,' she put in with unaccustomed sharpness. 'For a mere tenant, you do take liberties, don't you?'

He was silent, clearly weighing up possible answers, and just as clearly dismissing them all.

'OK, so I should have waited until you got back,' he said at last. 'Whatever—' his shoulders lifted again '—I seized on this as a stopgap until I get that computer.' He walked to the door, then walked back. He seemed once again to be struggling for the right words. 'Lauren—' he took her hand '—you'll have to trust me.'

She wanted to ask, Why? Why should I trust you? Instead she asked, 'Have you had breakfast?'

'Thanks, I'm OK.' He looked at his watch. 'I've an

appointment with a publisher in London this afternoon.'

Eagerly she asked, 'Are they going to publish your book when you've written it?'

'I'm a positive thinker. I can see no reason why they shouldn't.'

'That sounds a bit like arrogance to me.'

'Let's call it knowing one's worth, shall we? And if you're now going to call me big-headed, remember that for years I've earned my living as a journalist.'

'In other words, you know how to write.'

'That's about it.'

He removed the paper from the typewriter and put it with the other sheets. The words must have poured from him, Lauren reflected, judging by the pile he gathered together.

He snapped the lid on the old portable and made to lift it, then paused. Going to her and facing her, he pocketed his hands.

'Lauren Halstead,' he said softly, 'are you going to wish me luck?'

She was so pleased that underneath the apparent self-confidence there was just a glimmer of uncertainty, she put her arms round his neck and kissed him full on the mouth.

His arms tied her slender body to his, and he returned her kiss with a breath-robbing, intrusive one of his own. Her breasts were crushed against his chest, and his hips pressing against hers told her of male reflexes working overtime. She knew she would have dropped in a heap at his feet had he not held her so tightly.

Then he was free of her, gathering his papers, hauling the typewriter from the table and sprinting up the stairs.

Hands over her flaming cheeks, she fought the fire he had lit inside her, pouring the cold water of reason onto its flames. Breathing deeply, she told herself that

everything that had happened—was happening—
between them was because she was there, female and
available. As such, she had sparked his masculine
needs, and all his approaches, from his first kiss on, had
meant no more than that.

As she made toast and sat at the table eating it and
drinking coffee she heard him moving around upstairs.
The front door slamming and the roar of his car as he
reversed from the garage and sped away left her feeling
bereft and low-spirited, and dreading the empty day
ahead.

CHAPTER SIX

FOR some while that afternoon Lauren prowled restlessly, finally settling down to work. The ring of the telephone had her racing down the stairs. Oh, please, she thought, it has to be Brett, not Casey.

A woman's voice, husky, faintly sensual and supremely confident, grazed her ear. 'I would like to speak to Ellis, please.'

Instinctively Lauren felt that this particular caller meant trouble, although why, she could not fathom.

'Who?' Lauren answered. 'I—I'm sorry, but you have the wrong number. There is no one here by that name.'

'I wish to speak to Ellis,' the woman insisted, imperiously now.

'I'm sorry.' Lauren's reply was firmer and less polite in return. 'You have the wrong number.'

'And you are—?'

Lauren did not see why she should reveal her identity to a total stranger, but replied in a clipped voice, 'I'm the—' The what? she asked herself.

'The. . .?'

'The—the landlady.' It had been forced out of her by the woman's arrogance.

A tinkling laugh jarred Lauren's ear, at which she jammed the receiver back on its cradle.

Returning to her workroom, she seized a sheet of paper and began to draw, the swift, sweeping movements of her hand reflecting the anger that still simmered.

With a kind of wondering detachment she watched as Brett's face took shape in front of her eyes. For a few moments she stared at it, then threw down her pencil and made for the stairs.

She almost hurled herself into the garden.

Passing the brilliant blooms in the flowerbeds, ignoring the scents that filled her nostrils, she ran through the grounds and at last pulled up to a walking pace. She wandered slowly, studying each terracotta head, and finally she came to the one she was looking for and drew a sharp breath.

That particular head was of a man possessing features so like Brett's she could hardly believe her eyes, although the model for this statuette must have been a much younger man—a youth, in fact, not yet out of his teens. The resemblance was amazing, she told herself, and an enormous coincidence, but it just had to explain why she was convinced she had seen Brett Carmichael before.

Inside the house once more, she started back up the stairs when the telephone rang. Not that woman again, she thought, retracing her steps and lifting the receiver.

It was a woman, but clearly a much younger one.

'Would that be Lauren Halstead?' she asked. 'My name is Holly Dixon. Casey Talbert gave me your number.'

'Oh, hi,' Lauren greeted her, a smile in her voice.

'Casey tells me there's an exhibition of your paintings coming up soon. Is that right?'

Lauren assured her that it was.

'Well, I'm a clay modeller, and I wondered if you'd have any space available in the exhibition room for me to display some of my work too?'

Lauren hesitated only fractionally. 'I think that would be a great idea,' she answered. 'But it might be necessary for you to get Casey's uncle's permission—'

'He's already said yes,' Holly put in.

'Then why don't you come round? Bring some of your pieces and we can get going on a plan.'

'I'll be right there,' Holly replied excitedly. 'I only live ten minutes from Old Cedar Grange. See you.'

Lauren started again to climb the stairs, but this time it was her thoughts ringing all kinds of bells that caused her to return to the garden.

She was strolling from one terracotta head to the other when the scrape of bicycle wheels on the front drive had her hurrying to open the rear door. A long-haired, eager-eyed young woman dismounted, smiling broadly.

'Hi. Lauren? I'm Holly.'

A sweep of Lauren's arm welcomed the newcomer into the house. Upstairs in Lauren's studio, Holly praised Lauren's artwork and Lauren admired Holly's clay models, appreciating their shapes and accuracy of detail. They discussed the coming exhibition and began to draw a plan of Casey's uncle's gallery.

At which point Casey joined them, scraping his car to a standstill outside and yelling up, 'Anybody home?'

Holly was on her feet and halfway down the stairs. 'I'll let him in,' she offered.

'I was passing,' Casey said as he came into the workroom, 'so I thought I'd call in to tell you I've inserted a small paragraph in tomorrow's paper about your forthcoming exhibition.'

'Thanks a lot, Casey,' said Lauren, 'but I haven't fixed a date yet, and I've got loads to do towards it.'

'That's OK,' he answered. 'A little bit of advance publicity never did anyone any harm.'

'You'll need to have your pictures framed,' Holly told Lauren, resuming her seat beside her on the floor.

'You're right, Holly.' Casey crouched down. 'Anybody tell you, Lauren, I'm a genius at picture-framing?'

'He certainly is,' Holly supported him. 'It's his hobby.'

'Thanks, pal,' he responded.

'He's got a properly equipped workshop,' Holly put

in, carefully repacking her clay models. 'He does a really professional job.'

She glanced at the clock on the mantelshelf over the old fireplace, which was stacked with jam jars and brushes and other pieces of Lauren's paraphernalia. 'Heavens, I must fly. Glad to have met you, Lauren. I'll be in touch.' She smiled at Casey, then transferred the smile to Lauren.

'I'm just off too,' Casey said. 'If you like, Holly, I'll give you a lift.'

'Thanks, but I came on my bike. If you're wondering how I managed to stay upright, I strapped this box to the rear rack.'

No sooner had she gone than Casey preceded Lauren down the stairs. As they reached the bottom the phone rang.

'That instrument's alive,' Lauren grumbled, walking along the hall to silence it.

Casey reached it first. 'It's probably for me. I gave the office this number if they wanted to contact me.' He listened, his eyes swivelling to rest on Lauren. 'Yeah, she's here.' He held out the receiver. 'Your tenant. I forgot to ask how you were getting on with him.'

'OK, thanks,' she replied evasively. 'Hello, Brett.' She turned quickly, hoping Casey hadn't seen the light in her eyes. 'It was Casey, yes.'

Casey whispered in her free ear, 'Watch out, there's a thief about—of women's hearts. In the plural, lady. If he's beginning to mean that much to you...'

Lauren covered the receiver with her palm. 'Be quiet, will you?' she mouthed to Casey. 'And for your information, he doesn't—mean that much.'

'No?' Casey returned disbelievingly, and raised a hand. 'I'll be in touch.'

Brett's voice resembled arctic ice. 'He's keeping you company in my absence? Like staying the night?'

Lauren expelled a short, sharp breath. 'The answer's

no. But even if he were, it's none of your business, is it?' Brett did not reply. Lauren added, 'Is that why you phoned me—to catch me out with a man? Because if so—'

'I won't be back tonight. I thought it only polite to let you know.'

A shiver ran through Lauren at the implication. If a man who could kiss her and fondle her as this man had done could do something out of politeness and not warmth of heart, then from this moment on she must attach not an atom of meaning to anything that might happen between them. In fact, she declared silently, she would take good care that nothing did!

'Thank you for informing me of your movements, Mr Carmichael,' she returned crisply. 'But as a tenant, you're free to come and go as you like.'

She hoped the crash of the receiver against its cradle resounded in Brett Carmichael's ear. Then she wished she had kept her temper. After all, she was only his landlady, and as such she had no right to expect anything from him, had she? Not even politeness. . .

The next morning, she was called to the telephone yet again. She agreed with the caller that she was indeed Lauren Halstead.

'You won't know me,' the man went on, 'but I'm a local author. My name is Edward Hartingford. I've just seen mention of the exhibition you'll be holding soon in the town.'

'You have?' Lauren waited with interest.

'Ever since my retirement I've been hoping to meet an artist who would agree to illustrate a book I'm working on.'

Lauren's interest intensified.

'It's going to be called *Wayside and Woodland Birds*. Would you be willing to co-operate with me? I'd write the text, while you undertook to do the illustrations.'

It was too good to be true, Lauren thought. A

commission at last—what she'd been hoping, waiting for!

'I think I might be able to do that, Mr Hartingford.' She tried not to be too excited. 'As long as you're not in a hurry, that is.'

'Not at all, Miss Halstead. I understand that at the moment you're having to give all your attention to the preparations for your exhibition. I look forward to meeting you some time soon to talk the matter over and discuss details.'

The drawing of birds would be something new for her, she reflected, wandering into the library. Was there amongst Mr Gard's books one that dealt with the subject?

She found herself standing close to the section where, a few days earlier, she had spied Brett reading a book. As soon as he had become aware of her presence, she recalled, he had quickly replaced the book on the shelf, even though the subject he had been reading about had seemed to interest him greatly.

Her eye caught the merest hint of a bookmark protruding from the pages of a volume. Her hand pounced on it, but why it had been so eager to do so, she couldn't imagine. As a mere landlady, what interest did she have in her tenant's private concerns?

All the same, she argued, even though she knew a little more about him, he still remained in essence almost as much of a mystery to her as the day he had arrived so dramatically on the scene.

So she allowed her fingers to turn the pages until they reached the bookmark, which, as it turned out, was actually a folded letter. It wasn't the letter but whatever the text might contain that interested her.

The lines of print at that particular place dealt only with life and times in medieval England, which, in other circumstances, she acknowledged, would probably be worth studying. But had it really been that which had made Brett read its contents with such concentration?

As she closed the book the letter fluttered to the floor. In retrieving it, she saw that it was addressed to someone called Ellis.

Ellis? Hadn't that been the name of the person to whom the woman had referred in that short, but somehow acrimonious phone call yesterday? Which could only mean, couldn't it, Lauren reasoned, that a man by that name must once have lived in the house?

Before she could stop those intrusive fingers of hers, they had the letter opened up. Her eyes joined in the game and read—devoured, was a better description— the contents of that letter.

> Ellis
> I want you out of this house by tomorrow. You have betrayed my trust to such an extent that you have wrecked my life beyond redemption.
> I therefore intend to wreck your life so completely that you will never again be able to hold up your head in public, nor be able to pursue your chosen career without immorality and treachery being recalled in the minds of those with whom your work causes you to mix.
> You drove your mother from my life. Not content with that, you took away the woman I married in her place—took her from me in such a way that I can never regain her loyalty or love. Nor would I ever want to, because the child she has, she told me, was *yours*, not mine.
> I wish never in the whole of my life to see you again.

There was no signature after this grim and cutting ending.

With trembling fingers, Lauren refolded and replaced the missive. Had it been this that had caught Brett's interest, as indeed it had caught hers? In a strange way she herself felt reprimanded by it, although it had nothing whatsoever to do with her. Had Brett felt the same?

This man called Ellis must have been a total rogue, she mused. He must have left the house very soon after receiving the letter, as ordered by its writer so long ago. So why had the mysterious woman on the telephone wanted to contact him all these years later?

As Lauren closed the library door she remembered the reason she had had for going in there, but she decided to look up the subject of birds another time.

Brett had not returned so far that day, nor had he telephoned again. Which wasn't surprising, Lauren supposed, in view of the way she had talked to him before when he had called to tell her that his return would be delayed.

That afternoon Casey collected her to take her to Holly's studio, but first he took her to his place to show her with pride the workshop in which he carried out his picture-framing hobby.

'Isn't Casey a clever boy?' Holly asked of Lauren later, as she took them into the shed at the end of her parents' garden where she worked on her clay models.

'You seem to have everything you need here,' Lauren commented, looking at the kiln and the half-finished items spread over the wooden table.

'Courtesy of my mum and dad. They've been great in putting up with my mess, but suddenly they could stand it no longer and had this shed erected to accommodate it all.' She laughed. 'Casey helped me move my clobber out, didn't you?'

'Yep. How do you like her works of art, Lauren?'

Lauren ran an experienced eye over the moulded figures. 'Excellent,' she commented. 'They'll look just fine placed strategically among my artistic efforts. In fact, I'm wondering if they'll sell quicker than my pictures.'

'She's being very generous,' Holly commented with a smile. 'From what I saw of your work, Lauren, yours will fetch a higher price.'

For some time they discussed the approaching exhibition. Casey drew a sketch map of his uncle Henry's gallery and pencilled in possible display areas for both paintings and clay models.

They all drank coffee and consumed cakes which Holly's mother had made.

Finally Casey took Lauren home and stayed for a light meal, measuring some of her finished paintings and making notes in his reporter's notebook—which he never failed, he said, to carry with him.

After failing to persuade Lauren to spend the evening with him, he was on the point of leaving when the sound of a car braking in the driveway had Lauren racing to the window.

'What are you going to do?' Casey jeered. 'Fling yourself down the stairs to let him in? Lauren—' his tone held a warning note as she turned from the window '—your devotion to the mystery man who staged a dramatic collapse on your doorstep a week or so ago—'

'He didn't stage it, it was real,' Lauren objected.

'OK, OK. But your enthusiasm for the guy—it's showing.' He stood, sliding his ruler and pencils into his jacket pocket. 'I warn you, pal, there's not a faithful bone in that individual's body.'

'How do you know?' she asked angrily.

He held her shoulders. 'How? I'm male too, remember? And I'm an observer of men—not to mention women,' he added with a grin. 'I know a till-death-us-do-part man when I meet one and he isn't one. Lauren. . .' His hands slid down her arms to her hands. 'Johnny was right that night you-know-who made an appearance. Carmichael's got what it takes to make a woman fall headlong. Just don't fall, right?'

As he lifted her hand and put it to his lips the door

of her studio creaked, as it did whenever it was opened. Casey, his reporter's antennae springing into action, seemed to guess that they were being watched, and lifted Lauren's other hand to join the one already against his lips.

He did not release her, despite her agitated tugging, until the door creaked again, signalling the departure of the onlooker.

He clasped his own hands in a victory salute. 'One up to me,' he crowed. 'It's for your own good, Lauren. I'm off. See you soon for a session of framing.'

'You know all about framing, don't you?' came hotly from Lauren. 'You just had the pleasure of framing me, didn't you?'

'Pleasure's the right word,' he said with a grin, whistling as he descended the stairs.

If Casey had hoped to score a point against the tenant of Old Cedar Grange, Lauren concluded while walking quietly towards Brett's room, then he'd misjudged the situation.

That person had behaved like the tenant he was and closed his door firmly on the world. And on his landlady in particular, Lauren deduced, her spirits taking a dive.

How could she have been foolish enough to expect to find the door standing open, inviting her to go in and talk? About his hoped-for success with the publishers. . .about his search for a suitable computer— about any other subject that might have reinforced the fragile links between them after two seemingly never-ending days apart.

He did not emerge from his room until Lauren was preparing to go to bed. They met at the foot of the stairs. He nodded as if they were mere acquaintances. Which we're not, Lauren thought with a twist of anguish. We're more than that. . .aren't we? Or maybe, she corrected herself as she watched him make for the kitchen, it should be *weren't* we?

How could she bridge the yawning chasm that seemed to have opened up between them?

'Can I—can I cook you anything?' She addressed his back. 'Make you some tea? Or coffee?'

She stood in the doorway as he switched on the kettle.

'Thanks for your solicitous offer, but no, thanks.'

So he was still intent on freezing her out? Something drove her on. 'How—?' She cleared her throat. 'How—?' How did you get on? The question stayed in her head.

Starting again, she ventured, 'I—I had a phone call.' His raised eyebrows indicated mild, polite interest. 'A local author has offered me a commission. His name's Edward Hartingford. He'd like me to illustrate a book on birds he's going to write.'

'Good for you.' His tone was detached, clearly intended to convey uninvolved praise. He made his coffee, rested a hip against the wooden table and took a mouthful.

'It was Casey's paragraph in the newspaper about my exhibition at his uncle's restaurant that caught Mr Hartingford's eye.' Would the mention of Casey's name jog him out of his cold hostility?

He continued to drink, then slowly put aside his coffee-mug.

He straightened, hands in pockets, eyes narrowed.

'Why are you telling me this?'

She put her hands to her throat. It was as though a vice had fixed itself there, almost preventing her from breathing. Had he straightened out his thoughts while he'd been absent from the house—from her? Had he decided to build a wall so high between them that she wouldn't be able to scale it, even in her dreams?

Wildly she shook her head. 'I just thought you might be pleased for my sake.' Had he really taken her response to his phone call so badly?

He shrugged, and the vice closed even tighter at his coldness. 'It's none of my business, is it? Your words.'

She breathed again, but it wasn't easy. Maybe she had dreamt those kisses they had exchanged? Had she imagined he had felt. . .well, *something* for her? The pain of his rejection became so unbearable she could hardly stand it. So she fought back, hoping to hurt him too.

'So, OK. . .' Her head lifted proudly, her eyes defiant. 'It therefore follows that *I* don't want to know how *you* got on—whether or not the publishers took on board your idea for a book, or whether they chucked it out of the window and you with it. After all—' her heart was thumping '—I'm just your landlady.'

'When I called you, you were the one who put me in my place as a mere tenant,' he interposed calmly. So he had taken umbrage, after all.

'To you, I'm just someone to use,' she blundered on. 'To satisfy your *manly* appetite, even if only the fringes of it—a kiss or two. . .'

Her ears played back the provocation in her words, and as her brain applied the brakes her lips came to a screeching halt. Oh, heavens, what had she said?

His eyes flared and his hands whipped from his pockets. His jaw gritted and he took a stride towards her.

Her head went back and then forwards as his grip on her shoulders tightened unbearably.

'So what are you after?' came harshly from him. 'Doesn't Talbert *satisfy* you? Does he leave you wanting more—is he unable to oblige?'

'You're so wrong,' she got out. 'It's not like that between us.'

He was not listening. 'You want me to go beyond *the fringes* of my male appetite? You want me to take over from where Talbert left off and show you how it ought to be done? How a man *should* take a woman, give her what she wants and make sure she'll want more and more of it, hardly able to wait until next time round?'

'Of course—' She tried to add the word 'not', but it wouldn't come. Yes, she wanted him; she'd been longing for him to come back and kiss her again, kiss her senseless...

'You want more, do you?' he rasped. 'You want more than just my kisses? So be it, lady. We've got all night for me to show you how a real man makes love to a woman.'

His arms went round her, tying her to him, and his mouth came down, the pressure so great her lips gave way, allowing him access to the inner moistness. Her arms lifted to link around his neck, and she clung as he impelled her backwards, deepening the kiss until she felt that all control of her reactions had slipped from her and passed to him.

His arms had moved, and even as she gripped him his hands made their way beneath her cotton top, finding the softness of her shape and brushing aside the lacy covering that impeded the advance of his palms and seeking fingers.

A gasp was forced from her as the pressure of those fingers on her nipples brought waves of sensation flowing downward through her body. All the time the kisses went on, allowing her only seconds to breathe, then losing their lightness of touch to invade and advance yet again...

He released her suddenly and she nearly fell, but the pause was merely a preliminary to his sweeping her into his arms and carrying her up the stairs.

As he slid her through his hands to the rug beside his bed she swayed. Head back, she sought his eyes. He had switched on the bedside light, and in the subdued glow she saw what she had not wanted to see—a total lack of warmth, of loving passion, just a hard, driving male need. And anger. There was no mistaking it.

'No, Brett. This isn't the way I wanted it. I wanted—'

'Love?' he cut in mercilessly. 'You, a modern woman, want *love* with the sexual act?'

'Let me go,' she choked. 'Please.'

He released her so suddenly that the room spun, then slowly righted itself. This was a side to him she had never seen, never guessed at, and it frightened her. All right, so she accepted he didn't love her, but did he need to be so brutal about it?

She edged towards the door. 'I—I *hate* you like this. What happened while you were away that you've lost your human warmth, your pleasant nature? I wouldn't make love with you if—if—'

'If I *paid* you?' he cut in insultingly.

She shook her head, bewildered. 'The man who arrived on the doorstep that night wouldn't have said that. You've changed from the man I knew, the man I liked.'

'Oh, no, Lauren. You never knew me.' He ran his hand through his hair and she saw how tired he was.

If, at that moment, she had given in to her instincts, she would have run to him and drawn his head to her breast and comforted all that tiredness away.

Reason fought hard and won, and she went from the room, hands to her burning cheeks, wondering how they could possibly continue to share the same house after what had happened that evening.

CHAPTER SEVEN

IN THE event, it proved surprisingly easy to do just that. Lauren congratulated herself on her hitherto unknown ability to be in the same room as another human being yet ignore and tolerate being ignored by that person.

Brett seemed to have built a cocoon around himself—of silence, of apparent preoccupation with his thoughts to the exclusion, it seemed, of all others. Lauren concluded that this ability probably arose from the imprisonment he had suffered and the resulting deprivations—the clamping down on all his senses, his emotions, in order to survive the ordeal.

After a few days it began to get to her. It was not in her nature to be treated as if she did not exist, nor to treat someone likewise indefinitely. It bruised her feelings to such an extent that she found herself unable to concentrate or settle down to work, and she began to panic.

The exhibition, the dates of which had now been fixed, was moving nearer, and as she wandered into the living room three mornings later she wondered whether she would find the necessary incentive to enable her to finish her work in time, or whether after all it would have to be cancelled. But if that happened, she reasoned, she would be letting down both Holly and Casey, and that she could not do.

Standing at the doors which opened out onto the patio, she stared at the cedar tree beneath which it had all begun. She recalled the moment when Brett had first come into her life, and knew that she would never forget it. And it was then that she realised that, no matter what might or might not happen between them, she would never forget *him*.

It would be one-sided, because she also had to accept that without any difficulty at all Brett would forget her.

Tears came from nowhere, running down her cheeks. A sob escaped her, and she put a hand over her mouth to suppress all the others that were clamouring for release.

'Lauren.'

Hands rested on her shoulders and proceeded to turn her. She found herself looking up into a face so filled with compassion, so sympathetically warm, that her heart gave a leap of joy because the man she had come to know before his absence in London and their strangely bitter quarrel seemed to have returned.

'Brett!'

His arms went round her and her forehead pressed forward, finding a resting place against his shoulder. Her own arms moved around his back and the sobs slowly subsided. She felt—no, she knew for certain— that she had found a kind of sanctuary.

She also knew something else for certain. . .that she had fallen hopelessly and irrevocably in love with this man, Brett Carmichael, who had come in from the shadows.

His fingers found her chin and lifted her head, his gaze locking with hers, his eyes delving, seeking. As if, she mused dreamily, they were finding their way into her very soul.

'It's been terrible, Brett, treating each other as though we're total strangers.'

'For God's sake, Lauren,' he said hoarsely, 'you've been a million miles from me. Do you know what that did to me?'

She moistened her lips, moving to look up at him. 'You couldn't work?'

'Right.' A smile flickered across his lips, which proceeded to descend and settle on hers, seeming content just to rest there. Then they firmed and prised until her lips opened, and his tongue sought hers—hers darting eagerly to meet the hardness of his.

When at last he released her mouth her brilliant gaze met his, her arms linking around his neck.

'I couldn't work either,' she declared. 'Know what I feel now? I feel. . .liberated. All that terrible tension has left me.' Laughingly she disengaged herself.

'Lady—' his voice echoed her light-heartedness '—any time you need to use my embrace for medicinal purposes—' he opened his arms '—feel free.'

She laughed again out of sheer happiness. 'Would you excuse me, Brett, while I go and paint a master-piece? And,' she tossed back over her shoulder, 'you go and write one.'

She was halfway up the stairs when someone called from the vicinity of the kitchen, 'Anybody home?'

Lauren looked down. 'Casey. How did you get in?'

'Back door was unlocked. How else?'

Brett, still standing in the hall prior to following Lauren up the stairs, seemed to have turned back to stone. What was the matter with him? Lauren won-dered, spirits taking a dive. Didn't he understand that it was not Casey's presence that was filling her with artistic energy? That instead it was the breaking down of that terrible barrier between them and the reappear-ance of the warm feelings they had begun to share?

'I've just been filled with inspiration,' she told Casey.

'Yeah?' Casey looked from her to Brett, but plainly learned nothing from the action. 'I'll join you, then. OK?' He went up the stairs. 'I've come to measure up your stuff for framing.'

For some time they worked together in silence— Lauren painting as if her life depended on it, Casey measuring and making notes.

'Lunch?' Casey queried some time later, putting away his instruments and notebook. 'How about a snack at my uncle's place? They do a nice line in sandwiches on request. We can look over the gallery lay-out while we munch.'

Lauren nodded, putting aside her work with a satisfied sigh. She had progressed more that morning than in the past seventy-two hours put together.

'I'm sure I'll make the opening date on time now,' she told Casey as they descended the stairs.

There was the sound of a car revving for departure from the driveway. Lauren hurried to open the front door and ran to the driver's side.

'Brett.' Her smile was brilliant as she gazed in at him through the lowered window. Her eyes were met by an expressionless glance coupled with a curt nod.

'We're off to have some food and survey the exhibition area at Casey's uncle's restaurant.' Another nod. 'You're—' The curve of her lips began to straighten. What was the matter with him? 'You're planning to eat somewhere too?'

'Maybe.'

'I'm—' She turned on another smile. 'My brain's still inspired. My paintbrush—' she tried a joke '—seems to have grown wings, it's moving so fast over the paper. I'm sure it was your—our—'

His head turned briefly, no message in his eyes.

'Glad to have been of service,' was his brusque, unsmiling comment as he allowed his car to roll slowly down the drive.

The niggling feeling of worry was with her for the rest of the day, damping down the lingering sensation of pleasure. She couldn't mean *that* much to him, could she? So much that every time he saw her with Casey he became *jealous*? Anyway, hadn't she already told him that Casey was just a friend, nothing more?

Early evening, Casey saw her into the house, drinking the tea she had made him and staring through the living room window at the cedar tree and beyond.

'It dominates the garden,' he commented absently.

'No wonder the house is called what it is. Where's the man who came in from the cold under its spreading branches?'

She saw how Casey's mind had been working—the significance of the tree in the sudden arrival of Brett Carmichael into their lives, the strangeness of the nature of that arrival. . .

Lauren's shoulder lifted as she affected lack of interest. 'Working, I suppose. In his room.'

At once Casey pounced, reporter's antennae quivering. '*Working?*' he asked. 'On what?'

'He's writing. . .' Oh, God. Lauren's eyes fluttered closed, she had so nearly betrayed Brett's confidence. 'Writing letters, probably. Whatever.'

Casey nodded, only half convinced. '"Working" to me implies a job. If he gets one, either permanent or freelance, let me know, will you? Details like the name of the publication, newspaper or magazine—you know what I mean.'

Lauren knew, but thought, Oh, no, Casey Talbert. Not on your life will I give Brett's secrets away.

'Do you mean,' Casey probed, refusing to give up, 'he's writing letters *by hand*?'

'Well, I do know he found an old typewriter somewhere,' Lauren prevaricated, hoping she had put Casey off the scent.

He emptied his mug. 'Thanks a lot. Must go.' He lingered at the front door. 'Can't hear any tapping of ancient keys.'

'Ear-to-the-ground Talbert, they call him,' Lauren jeered, but was secretly concerned at Casey's unabated interest in Brett's affairs.

Casey challenged her. 'You know a lot more than you're pretending, don't you?'

'No, I don't,' she answered, bridling and feeling that his comment confirmed her fears. 'Anyway, even if I did—'

'You wouldn't tell me? Not even in return for me arranging this exhibition for you?'

'No, Casey Talbert, not even for that.'

He laughed, moving to kiss her, but she produced a cough, covering her mouth with her hand. Grinning at her subterfuge and raising his hand, he left.

Taking advantage of the togetherness between herself and Brett that morning and the right of access she felt that gave her, Lauren went upstairs and tapped on his door. Like Casey, she had heard no clatter of old typewriter keys. But that doesn't mean he's not working, she told herself.

'You want me?' was the cautious reply.

'Want' him? The connotations of the word started a tingling sensation deep within her, but she stilled it firmly.

'If you're too busy. . .' was her equally cautious response, putting her nose round the door.

'Come on in.'

His back was to her as she entered, but he turned, his glance going beyond her. 'Is Talbert with you?'

'Do you really think I'd let him see what you were doing? He'd be onto it like an eagle onto a mouse.'

His smile was touched with weariness as he watched her approach. He slid back his chair a little and she saw that in place of the typewriter she had expected on the somewhat cramped table he was using as a desk stood a small computer. Nearby, perched precariously on a chair, was a printer, a pile of paper beside it.

Brett's hand shot out, catching hold of her wrist and swinging her onto his lap. Her arms went round his neck and her longing for his touch made her respond with a depth of feeling that was beyond her control. His mouth found her throat, trailing kisses from her ear to beneath her chin.

'What are you trying to do?' she asked huskily. 'Trying to steal from me some of the inspiration you gave me this morning?'

He smiled, and as he put her from him she realised how preoccupied he really was with the task he had set himself. The impulse that had made him pull her to him and kiss her must have stemmed, she reasoned, forcing herself to be objective, not from any deep feeling for her but from a need to ease the tension that, in the writing of his book, had been building up within him.

His room had changed since she had last seen it. Books were everywhere—on the floor, on the bed, the dressing-table—while folders and atlases adorned his pillow, the washstand and even some opened drawers. On a stack of volumes stood an empty mug, placed carefully on a coaster.

'You obviously had a successful shopping trip this afternoon,' Lauren commented with a smile. 'Not to mention raiding Mr Gard's library.'

Expecting a smile in return, she was surprised by his answering frown. 'Any objections?' he asked, an edge to his voice.

It wasn't far beneath the surface, was it? she pondered. That hard side of him.

'None at all. No one else is using all the knowledge stored in it, so why not you?'

'Why not, indeed?' There it was again, that slight rasp which, curiously, seemed to reprimand—although Lauren could not understand why.

'You bought a computer,' she commented.

'I did.' He leaned back in the chair. 'A portable. It's small and compact. It's got everything I need.'

Its screen, Lauren noticed, held only technical data. He must have saved the contents as she'd entered, thus preventing her, or anyone else, from reading a single word of his book.

She walked to the window, looking down on the wide-spreading branches of the cedar tree. 'Were you successful?' she asked. 'Don't tell me if you don't want to, but did the publishers—?'

He laughed. 'They did. They liked my ideas so much they gave me an excellent advance.' He smiled mockingly. 'More than sufficient to enable me to pay the rent for the remainder of my stay.'

Portable computer? she pondered. *Remainder* of his stay? He couldn't—could he—be intending to move on in the not too far distant future?

Swallowing her intense disappointment at the thought, she commented, glancing round, 'It looks as if you need an extra room.'

'To work in?' He took in the near-chaos. 'Maybe I do.' Another devastating, mocking smile. 'Would you require extra rent?' He held up his hand. 'Before you correct me, would the *owner* require extra rent?'

His question, his sideways glance, flustered her. 'It never occurred to me. I suppose—I mean, Mr Gard might. . . No, he sounds such a nice man—'

'*Nice* man?'

'Oh, yes. I'm certain that in the circumstances he wouldn't demand it.'

'Do you mind which room?'

'Not at all. The choice is yours.'

They left his room and walked along the corridor together; he took a few steps into her workroom.

'This used to be Mr Gard's study,' Lauren informed him. 'Or so Marie told me.'

He nodded, lingering there so long that she thought he was inspecting her work, then it occurred to her why he might be looking around.

'Brett,' she said uncertainly, 'this is my studio.' She frowned at his strangely serious expression. 'If the. . . well, ambience of this room would help you work, I just might be able to find another for myself that's as well lit and roomy, but—'

He turned quickly. 'Thanks for the generous offer, but no, thanks. This room is most definitely not for me.'

She had to admit she felt relieved at his decisive

rejection of her offer. She was, none the less, puzzled by the resolute manner of that rejection. She left him still looking over the various rooms.

A card had come from Marie that morning, and in the kitchen Lauren idly read it again.

We're having a great time over here. Reggie's settling down in his new job and I in mine. We've rented ourselves a couple of rooms and we're both taking lessons in the French language. Hope you're coping OK, because whether you are or not—sorry, Lauren, but Reggie says not to give you a contact address because we don't want to be drawn into anything at your end. Hope you understand.

Love, an unrepentant Marie.

Wondering whether Brett had found a room that suited his writing needs, Lauren searched for him before retiring to her bedroom for the night.

Along the corridor a light spilled out from a partly opened doorway, and Lauren made for that, pushing the door slightly and peering round it. The computer and printer stood side by side on a desk he seemed to have found—probably ferreting it out from the back of a cupboard in the way he appeared to have discovered so many other things. A pile of printed-out paper stood on an upturned wastebin. His thoughts, it seemed, had flowed like lava from an erupting volcano.

'Hi,' Lauren said softly. Then she saw him.

His elbows were propped on the desk, the keyboard having been pushed aside, and his head rested on his hands. He was, she deduced, either in deep thought. . . or deep despair. She felt she dared not intrude, whatever mood might have hold of him.

Had she been his lover, or even just a close friend, she might have felt free to venture in and put her arms around his shoulders, stroke his hair, kiss his cheek, offering comfort and encouragement.

Since she was nothing to him—what were a few

HOW TO PLAY
SIX HUNDRED THOUSAND
BIG BUCKS
SIX HUNDRED THOUSAND
AND YOU COULD WIN THE
£600,000
PLUS JACKPOT!
YOUR PERSONAL GAME CARD INSIDE...
Mills & Boon®

◆ DETACH AND POST THIS CARD TODAY! ◆

EXCLUSIVE PRIZE Nº
CJ450150

BIG BUCKS

£

TWO WAYS TO WIN BIG BUCKS!

HURRY!
This jackpot must be claimed!

LUCKY CHARM GAME!

Claim up to 4 FREE books AND a FREE Mystery Gift!

scratch Here →

YES! I have played my Big Bucks game card as instructed. Enter my Big Bucks Prize number in the £600,000 Prize Draw and enter me for the Extra Bonus Prize. When the winners are selected, tell me if I've won. If the Lucky Charm is scratched off, I will also receive everything revealed, as explained on the back and on the opposite page. *I am over 18 years of age.*   10A6P

Ms /Mrs/Miss/Mr _____

                              BLOCK CAPITALS PLEASE

Address _____

_____

_____

_____ Postcode _____

MPS MAILING PREFERENCE SERVICE

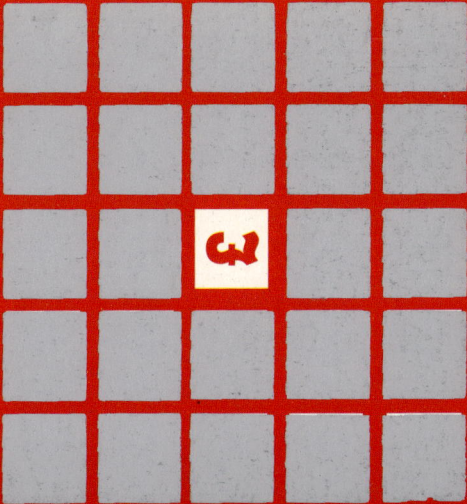

1. Uncover 5 '£' signs in a row... BINGO! You're eligible to win the £600,000 PRIZE DRAW!

2. Uncover 5 '£' signs in a row AND '£' signs in all 4 corners... BINGO! You're eligible to win the £30,000 EXTRA BONUS PRIZE!

THE READER SERVICE: HERE'S HOW IT WORKS

Accepting free books places you under no obligation to buy anything. You may keep the books and gift and return the invoice marked "cancel". If we don't hear from you, about a month later we will send you 6 additional books and invoice you for just £2.10* each. That's the complete price, there is no extra charge for postage and packing. You may cancel at any time, otherwise every month we'll send you 6 more books, which you may either purchase or return - the choice is yours.

* Prices and terms subject to change without notice.

The Reader Service
FREEPOST
Croydon
Surrey
CR9 3WZ

NO
STAMP
NEEDED

it to:- "Big Bucks" Prize Draw, Harlequin Mills & Boon, P.O. Box 236, Croydon, Surrey CR9 3RU - we'll assign a Prize Draw number to you. Limit - one entry per envelope kisses, after all?—she retreated soundlessly, wishing a hundred times over that she had had the right to go to him.

Something woke her in the early hours, and she sat up, listening in the darkness. Her first reaction was to thank heaven that she was not alone in the house, that Brett was there too.

Which could only mean, she deduced, that the sound that had disturbed her must have come from his room. It had been a kind of cut-off shout, and it had intruded upon her dream to such an extent that it had produced goose pimples all over her. It had, she was certain, been a cry for help.

It reminded her of the night he had arrived when, for the sake of her own sense of security, she had locked him in his room. He had been furious then. He seemed distraught now.

Swinging from the bed, she pulled a long-line sweater over her short nightgown. Pushing her feet into slippers, she let herself out into the corridor.

There was no light shining from his office now, so maybe he had accidentally locked himself into his bedroom and lost the key? Turning on the light, she sped along to his room and discovered that his door was unlocked.

Opening it, she noted fleetingly that the room was back to normal, all the equipment connected with his work having been removed to his newly acquired office.

Restless movements came from the bed and she padded across to his side, anxiety and a sleep-hazed mind breaking down barriers. She leaned across to stroke his brow, alarmed to feel moisture beneath her palm.

'Is it the fever again, Brett?' she asked. 'Do you want me to—?'

In the light from the corridor she saw his eyes come open, brilliant against his pale cheeks.

'You've come to me,' he murmured hoarsely. 'My dream girl has lost her ethereal, touch-me-not quality and taken on substance and form.'

His hand came out, fastening on her wrist.

'Dream girl', he'd said. The girl he'd dreamed up in his tortured mind, Lauren wondered, to make the terrible period of his imprisonment more bearable?

'Yes. . .' He spoke huskily. 'I want you. And yes, it's a fever. There's a burning fever upon me and it won't leave me until. . .' His voice died away, and she wondered if he was really awake, or still in his haunted dream state.

He turned onto his side, his eyes taking on a look of intense pain. In his imagination he was back, she was sure of it, back in the days of his past torment, his captivity by ruthless rebels.

'Stay,' he said thickly.

He believed she was part of his dream, her reason told her with clinical objectivity, her mere presence offering him a means of mental escape, a way of enduring the memory of the terrible hardships inflicted on him by his captors.

'Lie with me, dream girl,' he commanded. 'Here, beside me.'

He shifted, making a space on the bed, urging her down.

At first she pulled back, a warning voice telling her no. Why not? another, more reckless, voice asked. So what if the word 'commitment' isn't in his vocabulary? But it's in mine, she reminded herself. If I love him, and I do, I'll be the loser if I. . .

The sight of his hard body reached out to her, its outline beneath the cover suggesting that he wore nothing at all. Even as she looked down at him she felt a melting resolve not to give in to his wish. But weren't all her instincts warning her of the dire consequences to her future happiness if she did?

In the end he gave her no choice. He seized her

other hand and pulled her round and down until she
lay beside him. He gathered her into his arms and
pulled the cover over them both, closing his eyes and
bringing her face round until their breath mingled,
their lips almost touched.

I can sleep, she thought, in this man's arms. It's a
kind of sanctuary, lying here with him, safe from the
rest of the world... Safe with him... But not, she knew
as a few moments later he stirred, safe *from* him. Did
she, in her heart of hearts, *want* to be?

He turned her onto her back and in the half-light
stared into her eyes. Then he moved over her and she
let him. His hand slid beneath the layers of clothing
and she did not stop its exploration. When that hand
found her stomach, moulding it, stroking and moving
higher, she gasped, not in rejection, but in delighted
acceptance.

He grew impatient with the clothes she wore and
moved from her the quicker to remove them, tugging
them over her head and throwing them to the floor.
Her flesh rejoiced in the feel of him against her, all
barriers gone. Her heart hammered at the contact, even
as she told herself she was a fool to allow him to get
this far.

Although she had known him for a while now, and
even though she knew his name and his profession, this
man remained a stranger. He had come from the
shadows, and, a sombre voice told her, he would one
day disappear into those shadows.

It was no use, she would not heed that voice. She
was here in his bed, wasn't she? And it would have to
be a naïve woman indeed who thought it was mere
comfort he needed. Instead, it was a woman's body,
she reminded herself forcefully, and there she was,
unreservedly offering hers to him. Her heart hammered
at the contact, her feeling for him overcoming any
restraint that might have lingered.

She wanted to say, Remember me, Brett? I'm

Lauren, not just any woman, any willing woman you might have come across in your past life... But nothing came except quick breaths and soundless words from dry, tremulous lips.

He gripped her chin and stared into her eyes, then lowered his mouth to kiss them, one by one, moving down to find her breasts, using his tongue to tease until they tingled, to tug and nip until she gasped and writhed against the hard angles of his body.

Her fingers sank into the muscles of his arms, her toes curling in both ecstasy and pain as he stroked and caressed and scraped his hard fingertips over her burning, quivering skin.

She gasped again as those fingers took command of the core of her femininity, stroking and probing until she cried out, 'Please, Brett, please...?' He took her cries into his own mouth, intruding into the hollows of hers until she gasped again.

She longed to cry out, I love you, but she locked the words away in her mind, telling them they must stay in their hiding place forever.

As his exploring hands stroked her stomach her muscles clenched in spasms of pleasure. His palms followed the curving smoothness of her body and her senses caught fire, closing her mind to all the arguments—don't do it, don't let him—that her reason was still trying to get through to her.

When he moved onto her, his hard arousal brought her to an almost intolerable pitch of need. She knew then that the time had passed when she could tell him no. But what did it matter? she asked herself. She loved him, didn't she, so how could this be wrong?

He moved against her and she opened to him, her breath coming in gasps as he made a pathway into her most intimate self. Surrendering to the overwhelming joy of belonging to him entirely, she learned from him, following where he led, joining with him instinctively

as the increasing rhythm of his total possession took
her with him to the pinnacle of sensation and consum-
mate joy.

Dawn brought golden mists and rising bursts of
birdsong.

Lauren stirred, turning her head and feeling Brett's
regular breathing fan her face. His arm was across her
breasts in a gesture so possessive that a sense of
pleasure, closely intertwined with a strong feeling of
disquiet, took hold of her.

She had gone this far with Brett Carmichael. In the
enveloping darkness of the night she had given everything, all of herself, into his keeping. She sighed. Even
in the sober light of day, she couldn't find it in herself
to regret one moment of the time she had lain in total
abandonment in his arms.

He must have felt her moving since he too stirred
and pulled her closer, in his half-asleep state pressing
his lips against her shoulder and murmuring a name.
Hers? she wondered. Oh, let it be mine, she pleaded,
so that just for this once I can pretend he knew my
identity, and didn't mix me up with some woman from
his past who was part of his dream.

Savouring every second of the events of the night,
her spirits rose with the sun. The happiness that enveloped her at the wonderful memories she now shared
with him banished the doubts that had come from
nowhere and had threatened, curiously, to take hold.

Carefully she slipped from under his arm, finding her
slippers and shivering a little in the dawn chill. Pulling
on her layers, she crept into the corridor and switched
off the light that still shone there. In her room, after
showering, she dressed, then sped along to her studio.

Inspired, elated, she painted one picture after another,
the shapes and forms flowing from her brain and
through her hand onto the paper. Brett's lovemaking
had taken her to the heights—not just of passion,

but of her own artistic ability. Now she need have no
worries about completing sufficient paintings in time
for the show. In a little over an hour, she had produced
more pictures than in the whole of the previous week.

Her hand aching, she paused to stare out, seeing the
flowers' colours bloom brighter, hearing the birds sing-
ing with purer sounds, and felt more at one with nature
than she had ever thought possible. And all because
she had made love with the man she loved.

Even the young woman who looked back at her in
the mirror seemed a stranger, with more colour in her
cheeks, lips that were fuller, eyes more brilliant.

A voice broke the silence, and again it was so like
the shout that Brett had given when he had found
himself locked in that first night that she wondered if
his dream had turned back into a nightmare and he had
retreated into the past and was lost to her forever.

An awful apprehension gripped her, and she sped
along the corridor to his room, but he wasn't locked in.
In fact his door was partly open. Two strides and he
reached for her, pulling her through the doorway.

'Why the hell did you leave my bed without telling
me? Where in God's name did you go?'

Looking closely into his eyes, she saw that they held
the same torment as she had seen last night. She
realised then that he had been plunged back into his
days and nights of captivity, that he still had not
recovered from their effect on him and that the trauma
he had gone through still had him in its grip.

It therefore followed, her reason told her with a
chilling objectivity—and it tore her apart—that the
love he had made to her had not been to Lauren
Halstead, but to that 'dream girl' after all.

All the same, when he drew her against him and
kissed her, and gathered her to him and rocked her in
his arms, she banished her reason's warnings to the
back of her mind, letting the feeling of intense happiness take over again, lifting her high into the air until

once again she was treading cloud and stepping over sunbeams.

'Oh, Brett, dar—' Had she the right to use the endearment? She searched his eyes for distaste.

He shook her a little, and smilingly prompted. 'Dar—? Where's the rest of the word?'

'Darling,' she breathed.

'Say it again.'

'Darling Brett,' she whispered.

'And—?' He stroked her hair.

Excitedly she told him, 'I've been working and—would you believe?—I've turned out so many pictures this morning, I could use an exhibition room the size of the Albert Hall.'

His head went back in laughter. 'If that's what making love does to you, then. . .' He made to take her back to the bed.

She resisted. Something was making her hold back.

'Brett, I—'

'You—what?' He smiled. 'The urge to create masterpieces is still upon you and you want to get on?'

Eagerly she nodded. Thank heaven, she thought, that he'd offered her a valid reason. She smiled and went on her way.

How could she have told him the truth? she asked herself. That all her instincts had been telling her so far and no further?

The disquiet that earlier had darkened her happiness was creeping back. She had given him so much of herself, it had begun to worry her. Now the doubts had returned and were clamouring at the door of her mind, trying to break in.

Her reason was back to tormenting her: this affair, it said—if that's what has started between you—can only go nowhere. You've had your night of love, so call a halt now, while you've still a chance of emerging with only flesh wounds from your intimate encounter with this man.

Flesh wounds?

She loved this man so much that if she ever had to give him up—and her common sense was telling her there was no 'if' about it—it would shatter her heart, not merely break it.

CHAPTER EIGHT

LAUREN realised she was hungry when the aroma of toast and coffee drifted up from the kitchen. She put down the paintings she had just completed, and which she had been examining closely for imperfections, and raced down to find Brett seated at the wooden table.

The collar of his shirt was open, revealing a hint of dark chest hair against which, Lauren recalled with a warmth that enveloped her body, she had rubbed her face in the night. His casual trousers were taut across his hips, and she found she had to tear her eyes away as the memory of the feel of them against her own made her pulses race.

In one hand he held yesterday's folded newspaper, and in the other a slice from a pile of toasted bread.

Lauren inhaled exaggeratedly, then let her hand hover over the stacked, evenly browned slices. 'May I?' she asked.

'Go ahead,' Brett waved the plate towards her.

Her hand pounced and she took a hefty bite from the slice, chewing eagerly. Brett watched her for a few moments, then laughed.

'Don't bother. I'll say it for you,' Lauren managed through bulging cheeks, wiping her mouth with a tissue. 'Our night of love has improved my appetite as well as my artistic output. Isn't that what you were going to say?'

'I was going to say,' he returned, eyes raking her figure, 'how beautiful you're looking this morning.'

'What, in these old jeans and this ancient sweater?'

'It's not the outer wear that meets the eye, it's the memory of what lies beneath,' he added with a glint in his eye. 'Enticing, irresistible. . .' He made to put aside

105

the toast and the newspaper, but, laughing, Lauren backed away.

'Enough is enough—for the time being,' she qualified with a mischievous smile.

'Enough, lady, could never be enough where you're concerned.' He started to rise with intent.

'Oh, no,' she responded firmly. 'Everything's better for having to wait for it. Didn't you know?'

Running from the kitchen and up the stairs, she closed the studio door with a purposeful thump.

An hour later she heard the front door slam and paused, brush hovering, unable to believe that Brett had left the house without telling her. She looked at her own door as if willing it to open to reveal him standing there—then she saw the note which had been pushed underneath it. Dropping everything, she dived to pick it up, her pulse-rate increasing alarmingly.

> Dear Landlady. . .no, I'll rephrase that. My very dear landlady,
> Just to let you know I'm off for intellectual re-inforcements—that is, in search of more reference books to help me with my masterpiece. See you later.
> Yours, Brett.

The 'Yours' was underlined.

A car door was opened and Lauren raced to throw wide the window which overlooked the drive. About to get into the car, Brett tilted his head, almost as if he was expecting her to appear, and smiled sardonically.

'Message received, I see,' he quipped.

'Why didn't you come in?' Lauren reproached him disappointedly.

'Too much respect for your creative flow to interrupt it,' he shot back, settling himself into the driving seat.

His hand sketched an ironic salute as his car rolled away down the drive. Watching, Lauren felt that part of her was leaving with him.

The morning passed slowly. Each time the phone

rang Lauren dashed down, hoping quite without any real basis for that hope that it might be Brett. The first time it was Casey, asking how her master-works were progressing.

'Just fine,' she told him. 'I've been seized with an incredible burst of inspiration.'

'Yeah? Now, I wonder. . .'

'Wonder on.'

Lauren could almost hear his mind trying to work out a cynical and—did he but know it—correct explanation. But, merely promising another framing session later that day, he rang off.

The second call was from Edward Hartingford, the author with whom she had tentatively agreed to collaborate. He had, he said, noted the date of her exhibition, and looked forward to discussing his writing plans with her then.

Having concocted a hasty lunch, she returned to her studio, feeling the glow of the love she had shared with Brett in the night still lighting up her brain and imbuing her paintings with a deeper artistry than she had ever before discovered within herself.

Her thoughts tore themselves from the flowers they had been concentrating on and, looking through the window, her eyes followed the curving path of a bird in flight. If she really was going to collaborate with Mr Hartingford, she reflected, she had better do some research, hadn't she, into birds and their habitats? The idea excited her, because it would be a subject she had never studied before.

Stretching and yawning luxuriously, the wonderful languor from the night she'd spent in Brett's arms still with her, she wandered from her studio to pause outside Brett's office. The door to it was locked, and she passed it by.

The library proved to be an excellent source of information about birdlife. She took note of a volume which she felt would be of particular use to her when

she came to tackle the project offered by Edward
Hartingford, then wandered along the shelves, finding
herself drawn to the book which had as its bookmark
the strange and angry letter from one man to another
who had, it seemed, betrayed him beyond any possible
forgiveness.

A curious compulsion made her open that letter
again, and as she read the furious phrases a kind of
shiver took hold.

'. . .you have wrecked my life beyond redemption. . .
your immorality and treachery. . .you will never be able
to hold up your head in public. . .you took away the
woman I married. . .the child she had, she told me, was
yours, not mine. . .I wish never in the whole of my life
to see you again.'

Once more Lauren looked in vain for a signature,
finding none. With a puzzled sigh, she replaced the
letter and pushed the book back onto the shelf.

As she did so the back of her hand came into contact
with something that must have been a catch for, to her
astonished eyes, a whole section of those bookshelves
began to move. Her breath was momentarily trapped
in her lungs, her dry mouth opening on a strangled
gasp.

Hands on her throat, she watched as the book-laden
'door' pivoted to a right angle and creaked to a halt.
She waited a moment to see what else might happen,
then gathered her courage around her and took two
shaky steps into the room. As she did so she noted that
the stone walls were whitewashed and the ceiling low.

There was a faint aroma in the air of bread, which
implied, Lauren judged, still a little shaken by events,
that it must once have been the bakehouse. Against
the opposite wall was an antique table, while further
along stood a bureau. Venturing further in, she noticed
a stack of familiar-looking picture frames leaning
against the side of the bureau.

The shock of her discovery of the hidden room

receded a little as her recognition of the frames made her recall Marie's voice explaining why the three picture hooks in the hall were empty.

She glanced over her shoulder—was she still alone?—and crouched down to investigate, her hands beginning to shake as she stared one by one at the oil paintings.

The first was of a woman whose face she seemed vaguely to recognise, yet she was certain she had never seen the lady before.

The second portrait brought a deep frown to her forehead. It was not the sitter's stunning beauty that astonished her, it was the deep incision slicing across it that had her rocking on her feet. Scored through the line was the word 'deserter'.

Heart pounding, she turned to the third portrait, and this time a cry of horror was forced from her. The face was that of the man whose bed she had shared and with whom she had made love only a few hours before. He had been much younger then—perhaps fifteen years younger? A little older, perhaps, than had been portrayed in the modelled head of the same young man in the garden.

It was the desecration of this portrait—far worse than that of the woman's—that brought Lauren's hand to her throat and a terrible dryness to her mouth.

Gouged diagonally with a vicious blade across the face were the words 'seducer', 'villain', 'traitor'.

Kneeling now, and with trembling hands, she picked up the unspoiled portrait, and it came to her then whose face it was—that of the mother of the young man. Placing the three paintings on the floor around her, Lauren closed her eyes.

Marie's voice drifted back. 'Here hung Mrs Redmund Gard the first, and here Mrs Redmund Gard the second. . . And on this one, Uncle Redmund's son. The bad boy of the family.'

The young man, Lauren recalled, who'd had an affair

with his stepmother and thus had driven her away from his father... The son who had 'upped and left', or so Marie had said, 'never to be heard of or from again...' The Press had got hold of the story, and so out of revenge, his father had 'told the world of his son's many other amorous exploits...'

And the letter, that 'bookmark' letter that she, Lauren, had discovered, addressed to 'Ellis'... Ellis who? she wondered dully, picking up the badly desecrated painting and staring at the young man's face. No need to guess now who Brett Carmichael really was. *He* was Ellis Gard, son of Redmund Gard.

Other things came back to her—his words 'I belong...' on the night he had appeared on the scene and collapsed at her feet. The strange way he seemed to know where to find so many things in the house. His confident pronouncement that the owner's subject was history.

Those schoolboyish pieces of woodwork which he, Brett, had found in the garage, obviously lovingly kept by—at that time—a doting father. All this added up to one thing. All the time he had stayed there he had kept from her the fact that he really did belong—to the house, to the family.

'Lauren? Lauren!' The voice echoed through the empty rooms and she dropped the painting with a clatter.

She wanted to rewind the tape—backwards to the point where, after the phone call, she had left her work and decided to go into the library, to the point where none of this had happened. Then she would be able to welcome Brett Carmichael's return from the town, throwing herself at him and take his kiss, kissing him back until he...

'Lauren, for heaven's sake.' Then, more softly, 'Lauren?'

She struggled to her feet, heart pounding, and turned

to confront Ellis Gard, Redmund Gard's son and disinherited heir.

The sight of him standing there filling the opening of the secret door, hair slightly dishevelled as though in the course of his search for reference books he had run his fingers through it—that hair she had tugged at in her pleasure at the pain he had caused as he had entered her willing body only a few hours before—almost broke her heart.

Hands deep in the pockets of her painting apron, she stared rigidly at his face. Watching his smile fade as he took in the situation was like seeing the sun go down, never to rise again.

'G-good morning, Mr Gard,' she got out through dry lips. '*Ellis Gard.*'

'So—' his mouth twisted '—you know.'

'Now I know.' How she managed to keep the tremor from her voice, she couldn't guess. 'Why did you lie to me? *Why didn't you tell me who you really were?*' The anguish in her voice broke through her control.

'In all the circumstances,' he grated, 'I had the right to keep my true identity to myself. It's many years now since I've answered to the name Ellis Gard. Or acknowledged Redmund Gard as my father,' he added harshly.

He came right into the room and she backed slightly. If he came any nearer, she knew that her control would snap, and she would run into his arms and beg him to tell her that it was all a lie, that it simply wasn't true.

With a curl of the lip, he watched her retreat.

'This morning you loved me,' he sneered, his eyes raking her slender figure.

'I never said that!'

'But it showed, *Miss Halstead*. It showed.'

'Well, it was a false showing. Now I hate you. Do you hear? I hate you so intensely I could—I could—'

'Strangle me?' The curve of his mouth was a travesty

of a smile. 'Go ahead.' One step and he had her by the wrists, lifting her hands to encircle his neck.

The feel of him, his warmth, the drumming pulse in his throat under her moist palms, aroused such a rush of desire within her that she could not smother the cry that broke from her.

'No!' She tore away her hands and rubbed them down her apron as if they had been defiled. 'That— that letter—'

'So you found it in the end,' he responded coldly. 'I was aware that day I discovered it that you were trying to pinpoint that book on the shelves.'

Did nothing pass him by? she wondered, the shock of all that she had uncovered in so short a time still strong within her.

'Yes, Mr Gard, I found it. And I've read it. I know your true personality now.' And I know how you make love, she wanted to say—the wonderful way you made me feel last night, the way you made me part of you and you became part of me. . .

Never! her sensible self reminded her. Brett Carmichael—Ellis Gard—would never become part of any one woman. Remember what Marie told her about this man's 'amorous exploits' as she called them, and more, much more important, the love affair between Ellis Gard and his stepmother.

Inside her head a voice shrieked, Somewhere there's a son or daughter of his, living, breathing, walking around, aged maybe fifteen now. . .

'I noticed last night,' she hurled at him, knowing it was an arrow with a poisoned dart, 'unlike in your treacherous liaison with your stepmother, how you took great care that no other child would result from our—from our—'

One stride and his hands clamped onto her shoulders, his fingers digging mercilessly into her flesh. His eyes blazed, and his jaw thrust out as he shook her once, twice.

'Take care, my friend. You go too far,' he ground out.

Oh, God, she thought, his *friend*? After last night, is that all I mean to him? She knew that she had asked for his furious retaliation, but she did not regret one word. What she had said was true, and at the time, she had to admit, she had felt relief for his consideration sweep over her.

'It's true,' she protested as he released her, pocketing his hands. She rubbed her shoulders to restore the circulation. 'At the time I was so thankful for your thoughtfulness, but now I know the real reason for your caution. Once bitten, twice shy, the saying goes. No more unplanned offspring—'

He drew a sharp breath, teeth snapping. Then he pivoted and walked out, through the library and into the hallway.

She ran after him, throwing words at his striding, climbing figure. 'Once you told me to trust you. Now I know the truth, how *can* I trust you?'

She was talking to the air. He had gone into his room, having closed the door with a quiet firmness that told her she now meant no more to him than the landlady which, in reality, she truly was.

Retreating to her studio, she sat at her easel, hugging herself and letting the tears run wherever they wanted. The work into which she had poured her heart and soul only that morning stood all around, tormenting her.

The woman who had achieved that standard of near perfection—even she could see how good they were—had gone forever.

That afternoon she returned to the library, having abandoned all attempts to produce any more paintings that day—maybe forever, she thought despairingly, thrusting aside her paintbrushes and crayons. Nothing of any use would come. Her brain and her hand had decided not to co-operate. Her imagination seemed to have placed itself in a deep freeze, seemingly never to allow itself to thaw out again.

As a result of the catastrophic events of the morning she had forgotten to take the book on birdlife that she had discovered. Now, expecting to find the library empty, she jerked to a halt.

Brett's hand stilled on the page on which he was writing. His head lifted slowly and turned; his eyebrows were arched, his mouth a thin, unyielding line.

With another shock Lauren noted that he had moved the antique walnut table and chair from the secret room. One or two volumes were opened on it, while on the floor at his feet were piled three more. Of course he could move things around, she told herself, without either her permission or anyone else's. He belonged, she reminded herself. Oh, yes, he belonged; she knew that now. Much more, in fact, than she herself belonged.

'Yes?' His voice was cold, matching his eyes.

'A b-book—' Lauren cursed her voice for faltering '—one I discovered this morning. On birdlife.'

His brief nod seemed to dismiss her, and this rankled so much she stepped firmly across the stone-flagged floor, head high, and withdrew the volume, holding it tightly in her hands.

'What am I to call you now?' she heard herself ask, having really intended to leave the icy atmosphere of the room before it froze her to the spot. 'Ellis? Mr Gard?'

He dropped his pen and turned sideways in the chair, running his eyes over her. To her annoyance, her cheeks let her down, flushing a deep pink.

'My name is Brett Carmichael, as you well know.'

Her heart skipped a beat. 'You mean—' she was clutching at straws, at a lifeline that was made not of rope but of grass '—you're not Ellis Gard after all? You had a brother, a—a half-brother...' Her voice tailed off.

'I'm known in my professional capacity as Carmichael—my mother's maiden name. Brett happens to be my second name. Ellis Gard has not existed for fifteen years.'

So, she wanted to cry, who made love to me last night—Ellis or Brett? The traitor and the betrayer, or the honest, true, upright man I'd grown to love?

Face facts, she reprimanded her foolish self. They're one and the same, neither to be trusted.

Remember, too, that this man—yes, *this* man— Ellis. . .Brett—his true name is irrelevant now—has a child. . . She could hardly bear the pain that thought inflicted.

She cleared her throat. 'I suppose that now you— you've identified yourself as the son of the family, you won't want me here any longer.' She had to pause to steady her voice. 'My role as house-sitter has ended, hasn't it? I mean—'

'On the contrary. You're employed by my—' It was as if he could not bring himself to acknowledge the father-son relationship. 'By Redmund Gard. You're being paid to take care of his property. Yes?'

'Yes, but—'

'No buts. Tell me?' He stood, hands in pockets, aloof, heartbreakingly handsome. 'What makes you think I'm intending to stay on here?'

Her heart jerked. She stared at him. Oh, God, I can't take any more shocks today. 'You're leaving?'

He stared straight back, feet apart, gaze penetrating, piercing through to her very soul. It took him a few moments—or was it years?—to deliver an answer, and Lauren felt she could hardly bear it. 'I have no intention of staying in this house any longer than is necessary,' he said at last.

'Necessary?' she asked, uncomprehending. 'Necessary for what?' Her throat moved convulsively, yet with a mouth so parched she could not guess what it had found to swallow.

Silence greeted her question. Nor did his blank expression give her an answer.

'You will let me know in advance, I hope, so that—' She cut off the words. So that—what? It had been pure chance that Brett Carmichael had shown up when he did. If he hadn't, she would have been the only occupant of the residence.

He took her up, lip curling. 'So that you can make arrangements for Talbert to take my place? On a more, shall we say, *intimate* level, of course?'

Her shoulder lifted and fell. 'If that's what you want to believe, how can I stop you?'

The wheels of a car ground into the gravel outside. Lauren ran to the window, more to break the intolerable tension than out of curiosity. She had already guessed the identity of the driver. So, it seemed, had Brett.

'How touchingly glad you are to see him,' he commented cuttingly.

'He's doing a good job of framing my pictures,' she answered, then cursed herself for being so much on the defensive.

'Yeah?' Brett resumed his seat. 'Up and coming investigative journalist that he's trying to be—just make sure he doesn't *frame* you.'

His tone was so dismissive Lauren could not decide whether work was on his mind or whether he really was glad to get her out of the room.

'Hey, these efforts really are great,' Casey exclaimed, gazing at Lauren's collection of flower studies propped against the furniture in her studio.

'I'd say inspired,' Holly Dixon commented, lowering to the floor the cardboard box containing her own work.

'What got into you, Lauren?' Casey queried, his smile faintly suggestive.

I could tell him, she thought, but nothing will drag that from me.

'You know,' she responded half jokingly. 'It was one of those mornings when the joys of summer get into you and bring something really good to life inside you.'

'I know the feeling,' Holly confirmed with a smile. 'I get it sometimes with my work.'

'Maybe it's like the feeling I get,' Casey conceded, 'when a good story pushes itself in front of me and only me, so that I'm onto a scoop.'

Lauren glanced at him, searching for a hidden meaning in his eyes. I'm just too suspicious, she told herself, probably because of Brett's warning this afternoon.

As Casey assembled his tools Holly unloaded her figurines, each lovingly wrapped in newspaper. She spread them around her, and pushed the box out of the way. She was examining her model of a peasant girl with a bird nestling in her arms when a sound from the doorway had them all looking up.

Brett stood there, regarding the trio with a half-smile. Lauren, whose heartbeats had assumed their customary race against time, could discern no mockery in his expression, just a kind of questioning interest.

'Hi,' said Casey, assembling pieces of wood.

'Oh, hi,' echoed Holly, plainly hoping that the very masculine male at the door might actually join them. 'You arty-crafty too?'

Lauren remembered that Holly had never met her tenant—yes, on consideration, he still *was* her tenant— and found herself bristling with a quite ridiculous jealousy at the warm welcome in Holly's eyes.

'No. I just live here.' Brett's eyes slid to Lauren, clearly amused at her attempt to keep her colour and her embarrassment under control.

Holly looked at her too, eyebrows raised in query.

'This is Brett,' Lauren explained flatly. 'Brett Carmichael. He's a tenant—of Mr Gard's. Not mine, of course. I'm just the house-sitter, as you know.'

Holly nodded her acceptance of the situation, her mind instantly switching back to her work. To Lauren's surprise, Brett did come in. He strolled across to join not her, but Holly, crouching down and handling her figures with a deep interest.

'These take me back,' he commented. 'On my travels I came across tribes who fashioned figures out of wood, or chipped at stones. Don't get me wrong—' he directed a winning smile at the models' creator '—I'm not implying that yours are primitive. In fact, some of them are very modern.' He picked up the peasant girl. 'This, of course, being one of the exceptions. I can see they've come from the heart.'

He ran his fingers over the figure's shape and, to her horror, Lauren found her own body's responses coming to life—as if *hers* was the body his hands were touching, caressing, arousing. . . When his eyes flicked to hers, she cursed the heat that had arisen, warming her throat, her cheeks, firming her breasts.

He smiled as if he knew what was happening to her, putting aside the figure and rising, hands thrust into pockets.

The telephone rang, and Lauren had to brush past him to get to the stairs. Turning before she descended, she saw that he was standing in the corridor, watching her with narrowed eyes.

She paused. The whole situation had changed now, hadn't it? The house was his to live in, love in, work in, and therefore the telephone was his to answer.

'I'm sorry,' she said politely. 'Perhaps it's you who should take that call?'

He stared stonily back at her.

Giving up, she raced down and said into the mouthpiece, 'Yes? Can I help you?'

'I should hope so. I wish to speak to Ellis,' the woman caller replied.

It was that voice, the tone as imperious as before!

The difference, Lauren told herself bitterly, was that now she knew exactly who Ellis was.

'Don't try telling me this time that he isn't there,' the woman continued unpleasantly. 'He contacted me himself, giving me this number. Tell him it's Imogen—Imogen Gard.'

Lauren turned, finding Brett beside her. Without a word, she offered him the receiver.

'Imogen?' He knew without being told. 'I'm glad you called me. Can we meet? Yes, as soon as possible. Is Elissa with you? Of course, she's at boarding-school. So we'll be alone. Good.'

Lauren fled up the stairs, back to her friends. Heart at rock-bottom, as though it had plunged over a cliff, she thought, Their child's a girl—Elissa. Named for her father—who else?

She should have guessed. All man that Brett Carmichael was, he did have a female in his life. What was more, it was still the same woman. Which, after all these years, just had to mean that he still loved her.

Imogen Gard. The woman with whom, when she had been his stepmother, he had had an affair. And by whom, quite shockingly, he had a child.

CHAPTER NINE

IT WAS almost dark when Lauren arrived back at the house that night. Another car was parked alongside Brett's, and her heart, which she had thought couldn't sink any lower, went through the floor.

Even if an opened envelope left carelessly on the passenger seat had not carried the name 'Mrs Imogen Gard', there would have been no need to take a guess as to the identity of the owner of that vehicle. Her perfume lingered in the hall as Lauren let herself in. It led, she noticed, in the direction of the living room, which meant that that room had to be avoided at all costs.

Lauren made for the kitchen. Having eaten a scratch meal at the gallery where she, Casey and Holly had spent the evening preparing for the show, she made herself a coffee and carried it up to her studio. Her mind was too active for bed.

Skimming through the book about birdlife which she had discovered in the library, she made a few pencil sketches, then listlessly put them aside, going to the window and staring down in the light of the moon at the cedar tree, and calling back to life the night Brett had appeared in the garden.

Her gaze switched to the paved area below, and her heart thumped as Brett and his guest wandered out into the moonlight. For the first time she saw the woman in Brett Carmichael's—or was it Ellis Gard's?—life.

Made mysterious by the silver of the moon, the woman closely resembled the desecrated painting which had been hidden away in the library. The fifteen or so years that had passed since the artist had carried

120

out his—or her—undertaking had not deprived the woman of her good looks.

Tall, slender still, she would, Lauren decided unhappily, be a tempting morsel for any man. The colour of her hair, made paler by the soft light, had clearly been taken in hand, and her dress fashioned to emphasise the slimness. Who could win, Lauren asked herself sadly, against such sophistication? Especially when that woman had borne the child of the man in question?

Heads almost touching, as if they were whispering, they seemed to be deep in discussion. Lauren despaired at their obvious closeness. Unable to stand the pain that closeness was giving her, she moved from the window, deciding at last to go to bed.

Even as she tried to sleep her imagination played on the two figures in the garden. In her fevered thoughts their lips met, their bodies entangled. She slipped into a dream and they followed, two figures clinging, becoming again the lovers they had once been. . .

She opened her eyes to the lightening of the sky. Dawn was on its way and the birds were in splendid voice. Their very cheerfulness made her aware of how low her own spirits were.

No doubt Brett had his lady-love beside him where she, Lauren, only twenty-four hours before, had lain so sublimely happily in his arms.

To escape from the picture her tortured imagination had conjured up, she turned her mind to her and Holly's approaching show. Last night, as she had looked around at the display which she and her friends had been building up, she had had the feeling that something important was missing.

At the exact moment when the bedside clock told her how early it still was, her subconscious mind told her what that something missing was. She swung from the bed, showering and dressing in record time.

Rummaging in a drawer in her bedroom, she found her camera, slung it across her shoulders, then crept down to the kitchen. She made a flask of coffee and packed a couple of rolls from the fridge.

As she emerged through the side door it dawned on her that the visitor's car was missing. Her heart leapt at the thought that after all Brett might have slept alone, but she shook her head at its naïvety.

Cool reason told her that Imogen Gard had probably hired the car, and that Brett had accompanied her in his own car back to whichever hiring agency she had used and had brought her back to the house.

Turning her own car in the direction of the hills, Lauren drove towards the rising sun, feeling her spirits struggling valiantly to rise with it. She parked off the road, swung her small backpack into place and walked.

She photographed summits and valleys, forest-covered hills and grazing sheep, then walked some more and took pictures of craggy rocks, sloping fields, wandering hedgerows, snapping the beauty around her as if her very life depended on it.

Now and then she would drink some coffee, munch a piece of roll, then dust her hands and start again. It was not until she had refilled her camera with a fresh film and started using it that she noticed through her lens that the majestic white clouds had grown darker. The sun's warmth had disappeared, and rain not only threatened, it had arrived.

Pushing her camera safely away, she made for the car. In her hurry she had forgotten to bring a jacket, and now, as small raindrops grew larger and more frequent, she regretted it.

As she battled through trees and climbed over stiles she felt the rain soaking through her clothes, but she told herself she didn't care. She had found the way to bring more life and meaning to the art show—and worked off some of her misery.

At least, she thought she had, until she ran through the downpour to dive into the house, making for the warmth of the kitchen and turning to discover that the door was being held open for her by a man who badly needed a shave and whose jeans and jersey looked as though they had been tugged into place by furious hands.

He had indeed spent a hard night with his lady-love, Lauren thought with unaccustomed and bitter cynicism. But his anger—through frustration at his bedtime companion's departure, maybe?—was directed at her, Lauren.

'Where the *hell* have you been?' he greeted her. 'Passed a busy and eventful time in Talbert's arms? Couldn't he wait until he got you under cover, and it rained all over your—activities?'

'You can talk,' she hurled at him. 'Accusing *me* of lecherous activities when *you've* been indulging in debauchery all night.'

He looked puzzled. 'Debauchery? With whom?' She knew his raised eyebrows were intended to intimidate, and they did.

'With—with your lady-friend. Imogen Gard. Isn't that her name?'

'It is?' His jaw thrust forward, his teeth snapped. 'Before we get deeper into this intriguing discussion, you'd better strip and shower—unless you intend to develop pneumonia?'

'I'll do what I want,' she retorted pettishly, and deliberately ran a slow hand over her soaking hair.

One step and he was in front of her. 'If you meant to provoke me, you've succeeded.' He swung her up and into his arms, striding up the stairs with her, her kicking legs and struggling body making no impression on him. Her demands to him to leave her alone and put her down bounced off his gritted, bristled jaw.

Setting her on her feet, he pocketed his hands and eyed her dishevelled state. 'Now,' he gritted, 'do you want me to do the stripping for you, or will you see sense and fill that bath?'

Undaunted, she looked at her watch. 'I haven't time. I must go to the shops and get my film developed. I—'

'Film? What film? Some great shots you'd have got in this weather.'

She shook her head. 'Very early it was sunny and warm.'

'Which is why you were stupid enough to go out without a jacket? Or—' his eyebrow raised '—were you in such a rush to keep your assignation with Talbert?'

'I *did not* meet Casey. *Will* you believe me?'

'OK.' He leant against the doorframe. 'I'll bargain with you. I'll believe you if you'll believe me. I slept alone.'

Something inside her relaxed, like a fist uncurling, but she needed reassurance. 'What if *sleeping* didn't come into it?'

His eyes narrowed. 'You really are a little. . .'

Her fingers were turning her blouse buttons without unfastening them. She was darned if she'd undress in front of this cynical hunk of masculinity.

'You want me to do that for you?' Without waiting for an answer, which he clearly knew would be in the negative, he reached her, brushing aside her fingers, and he had the blouse open and off her shoulders before she could stop him. 'Now these.'

Fuming at his audacity, she reached out to beat him off. But he was releasing the waistband of her trousers, and before her astonished hands could prevent him he was peeling those trousers over her wriggling hips and down to her stamping feet.

Almost naked, she crossed her arms as best she could over the remainder of her clothes, which were skimpy in the extreme.

'Go!' she cried. 'Get out, will you?'

If his hands touched her as seductively as his eyes were caressing her, she would be lost.

His hands did come out, and she backed away, but the bathroom was not large and she soon came up against the washbasin, with no prospect of escape from that.

His hands closed around her bare waist and then gentled, moving upwards to cup her breasts. If he'd gripped her, she thought, it might have aroused her anger and she would have fought him off, but the light, skimming strokes that feathered her skin brought a shiver to her body and a feeling of weakness to her legs.

Then she was in his arms, her bra unaccountably falling away while his mouth hit hers, prising open her lips. His tongue went on a voyage of rediscovery, making free with every corner and hollow his tongue found there, while his hands made themselves familiar again with the slender curves of her hips, her thighs, her femininity that she had offered him so freely—and, yes, she thought dazedly, so wantonly—the other night.

The pads of his fingers were sliding their seductive way beneath her briefs, and she, to her shame, was making no attempt to stop him. And then came the sound of wheels moving slowly along the drive—too slowly, Lauren thought hazily, arms locked around the neck of the man who was deliberately seducing her, for it to be Casey.

'A visitor,' she got out, tearing her mouth from his. 'Not mine—yours. Your lady-love, your woman—it must be her.' She groped for the towel and wrapped it round her in a futile attempt to hide her burgeoning breasts and regain her poise.

She tossed her head, angrily aware that her colour was as high as her pulse was racing. 'Come back for more, probably, of whatever you gave her last night.' He looked tautly back at her, giving away nothing. 'I expect you enjoyed h-her—' she cursed her faltering voice '—more than you did me. She's more experienced, more—more mature.'

The bell downstairs clanged, thumps following, and a voice was raised. 'Hi there, Ellis. Let me in, will you?'

'You see.' Lauren's head lifted triumphantly, even though her heart sank in despair. 'I was right. She must have stayed locally after—after you made love. Right again?'

His mouth was a thin line as he opened the bathroom door. 'You'd better have that bath,' he directed grimly.

Only when Lauren had heard him go down did she turn on the taps, her tears mingling with the steam, her sobs lost in the sound of the running water.

Emerging some time later, dressed again, Lauren found that she could not avoid passing Imogen Gard in the corridor. Brett was behind her, shoulder propped against his doorframe, hands in pockets, wearing a sardonic smile.

There was no doubt about it, Lauren reflected, Redmund Gard's second wife—*ex*-wife—was elegance personified, from the top of her coiffured head to her fashionably shod feet. Her dark suit just had to bear a couture label, also the white blouse with its mandarin-style collar, though a silver-crafted figure at its neck softened the severity of the outfit.

Imogen half turned towards Brett, but, Lauren guessed, she was really addressing her. 'You don't really want me to go to a hotel again tonight, do you, darling?'

Brett did not respond.

'I'm sure your *landlady*—' now she turned to Lauren '—that is correct, Miss Halstead? I believe that is how you once described yourself to me?—could provide me with a spare room while I'm here.'

For heaven's sake, Lauren thought, how long is she staying?

'I'm no longer Mr Carmichael's landlady,' she retorted. 'Nor am I an innkeeper or chambermaid.' There came a sharp intake of breath from Brett and a faintly injured recoil from his visitor.

Head high, Lauren continued to address Brett. 'You know you have the right to give Mrs Gard any room you like. Correction, any room *she* likes. You also know where all the bed-linen is kept, and anything else she might need.'

Feeling she had won some kind of victory, Lauren proceeded to her room, hearing Imogen whisper, 'She knows, then?'

'She discovered the letter.'

'The paintings?'

'Those too.'

'Oh, my God.'

Lauren closed the door on the conversation, leaning back, head touching its hardness. For the first time in her life she had been rude, deliberately so, to a perfect stranger. With a shrug, she combed her hair, tidied the bed and closed the door behind her.

In the kitchen she took her camera from the table and let herself out into the weak sunshine that had followed the downpour. She drove into town and left the film, saying she would pick up the prints in an hour, then drove on to Chez Talbert.

Casey's uncle Henry unlocked the door of the restaurant and greeted her warmly.

'It won't be long now, my dear, will it?' he remarked as she mounted the stairs to the gallery.

'It's certainly taking shape,' Lauren replied with a smile that she produced from somewhere. Her spirits, which should have been high, were at floor level.

Henry studied the poster which he had allowed to be placed near the entrance. 'My goodness, only two more days.' He smiled, nodded and walked busily away.

Lauren strolled round the extensive display, admiring Holly's pottery and liking the come-view-me angles of the stands which Casey had constructed. It hit her with some force that the feelings she'd had about the missing 'something' from the display were fundamentally correct, and was glad she had acted on impulse that morning and taken those photographs.

Deep down, she was still troubled, and it didn't take

her long to discover the cause. There was a payphone in the entrance hall downstairs and as she inserted the necessary coins her heart stepped up its beat.

When Brett answered, she inhaled deeply and identified herself, then spoke the lines she had been rehearsing.

'Will you please convey to your—to Mrs Gard, my apologies for being so impolite towards her?'

The response was a long time in coming. 'And?' Brett queried.

'And—well, that's it.'

'It wouldn't have been a touch of—shall we say—greenery which caused that outburst?'

'Jealousy?' Lauren burst out. She could almost see his cynical smile. 'Of whom? Of what?' She was all the more annoyed because she honestly had to concede that Brett was right. 'You forget that I now know all about your immoral ways, your dissolute past. You think I care a damn about you any more?'

'My God, my father did his work well,' she heard him snarl just before she slammed down the receiver, annoyed that she had not been able to eliminate the tremor from her voice before she had disconnected.

As she left she sought out Casey's uncle. He emerged smiling from the catering area.

'About the eats for the show, Mr Talbert,' she said. 'Not to mention the drinks—'

'All arranged, my dear. Compliments of the house.'

'Are you sure, Mr Talbert?' Lauren asked on a gasp. 'I mean—'

'Your art show will bring me extra custom, Lauren. For that I'm most grateful. I've arranged it all with Casey. And you never know—' he gave her a warm smile '—you might gain financially yourself. Just as long as you don't label every one of your works of art with those maddening initials "N.F.S."'

'Not for sale?' Lauren smiled. 'Don't worry, Mr

Talbert, I'll willingly sell the lot, then get down to producing some more while the art show lasts.'

'Instant masterpieces, my dear? That's the spirit.' Henry Talbert chuckled to himself as he went on his way.

Lauren drove back to town and collected the prints of her morning's photography session, then hurried home to get down to her painting.

As she made to use her key the entrance door started to open.

'Don't worry about the cost,' Brett was saying to his guest. 'Refer the hotel bill to me. And about Elissa's school fees—of course I'll continue to pay them.'

Imogen saw Lauren first. Lauren noticed how her foot nudged Brett's, silencing him.

Lauren raised expressionless eyes to his. 'Did you find Mrs Gard a room to her liking?' she asked.

'Thank you for your offer, Miss Halstead,' Imogen responded, her expression disdainful, 'but I prefer the *welcome* of the hotel management—impersonal though it is—to your grudging one.' With which crushing statement she swept past Lauren to her car.

Lauren made for the stairs, unaffected by the attempted put-down. Instead, her mind was going round in circles at the fact that Brett, clearly having acknowledged that Imogen's daughter was also his, was bearing the cost of her education. And heaven knew what else, Lauren thought disconsolately.

Sorting through the colour prints, she tried to put her unhappiness behind her, worried that it might come through into her painting.

Troubled by the shortage of time before the official opening, she drove herself on. And by the end of the afternoon she had surrounded herself with the end products of her efforts, feeling a glow of satisfaction at all that she had achieved.

Brett followed her downstairs as she made for the

hall telephone. As she dialled he turned, observing her closely.

'You've painted yourself,' he commented with a half-smile, approaching her. He took the rag damp with solvent which hung from her apron pocket and started to wipe the paint smears from her cheeks and forehead. It was an action springing from an intimacy which, she told herself fiercely, did not exist any more, and it disturbed her unduly.

She snatched at the rag just as the call was connected to Casey's desk. There was a kind of tug-of-war, but Brett's grip was so strong that Lauren gave in and did her best to concentrate on the phone call.

'Hi, Casey,' she said, 'guess what?' Two arms were reaching round her waist. 'I've got a pile of—'

One over-familiar hand was invading her apron pocket, while the other was pushing the paint rag back into place.

Lauren gritted her teeth at the feelings Brett's provocative action was arousing and twisted away to free her body from the octopus-like arms that were imprisoning her.

'Go away,' she whispered hoarsely.

'Who, me?' Casey queried. 'But you've just called me.'

Lauren turned pleading eyes to her tormentor. 'Do this to your lady-friend, not to—'

'What are you talking about?' came Casey's puzzled voice. 'What lady-friend? The only female who might come into that category where I'm concerned is a girl called Lauren Halstead, and she—'

'I wasn't talking to you, Casey,' Lauren answered in a strangled voice. She closed her eyes in relief as Brett released her, making his mocking way upstairs.

She cleared her throat loudly, at which Casey drawled, too knowingly for Lauren's comfort, 'Got a frog in it, have you?'

'Sorry, Casey. As I was saying—'

'Before you were so rudely interrupted by. . .?'

She did not take him up on his leading question.

'I've done a load more work. It all needs framing. Could you oblige in time for the art show? I know it's only a couple of days away—'

'*More* work? But why? You already had plenty to offer.'

'I'll explain this evening. That is, if you can come then? I know it's a rush job, but—'

'Just call and I'll come, Lauren. Right?'

As she rang off Brett descended once more, mockery still curving his mouth.

'Why did you do that?' Lauren demanded. 'Is it a habit of yours to make physical—and I do mean *physical*—contact with every woman in sight?'

He made no reply. Hurt feelings made her add with a touch of spite that was foreign to her, 'Wasn't your day with your *lady-friend* sufficient to satisfy your male needs?'

He reached the door without answering. In his hand was a briefcase which, Lauren judged, bulged with items other than printouts of his manuscript—like clothes, toilet articles. . .

'Where are you going, Brett?' He made for his car and she ran out. 'All right, so it's not my business,' she called after him. 'But at least you could tell me how long you'll be away.' To her annoyance, a pleading note was interwoven with the words.

Reaching his car, he answered, 'Who knows?'

'Brett. . .' She was pleading again, but she couldn't help it. 'My art show. . .had you forgotten? Aren't you coming?'

He looked at her then as she stood a few paces away. A curious expression crossed his face but all he did was repeat maddeningly, 'Who knows?'

As he unlocked his car Casey drove up, parking beside him. The two men exchanged glances, and Lauren had the feeling that a silent war had been declared. Brett's eyes switched to Lauren. The look in them told her exactly what he thought of her. Two could play at that game, she thought furiously, but by the time she could think of a crushing comment, he had driven away.

'So our mystery man's got a girlfriend,' Casey commented a little later, eyes on his work.

It was not a question, Lauren decided, which meant that it did not require an answer—although she groaned inwardly at the thought that she had inadvertently given away something which would have been better kept secret. Especially from Casey, whose appetite for titillating items to write about was insatiable.

To Lauren's annoyance, Casey had plainly taken her silence to mean yes.

'Ever met the lady?' he probed. He did not accept Lauren's lift of the shoulder. 'You can't deny he's got one. I heard you mention her when you called me earlier.'

'OK, so he's got a girlfriend.'

'Tell me something,' he went on, using glue with care, 'what does he do for a living.'

'Living?' She honestly didn't know.

'Yeah, living—like having the means to pay the rent.'

'He's not—' She swallowed a gasp. Not a word must pass her lips about his true status, nor about the book he was writing—especially to Casey. 'He—well,' she invented, 'I guess he has private means, don't you? Perhaps he's living on his savings, hmm?' She pretended to be admiring Casey's handiwork.

'Yeah.'

It was a disbelieving sound, and Lauren guessed his reporter's curiosity had been fully, and worryingly, aroused.

Dressing for the official opening of the art show, Lauren had to swallow her disappointment at Brett's continued absence.

As she pulled on a long black skirt she twisted to see how much of her leg its dramatic slit revealed, then shrugged uncaringly as she saw that a large portion of her thigh also peeped through.

Her long white sleeveless top was even more daring, the intricate stitchery down the edges barely meeting from neckline to hem. Its tiny buttons were fastened with loops that scarcely closed the gap, not quite hiding the soft, smooth flesh beneath, and the cleft between her breasts would play hide-and-seek with whoever came near enough to see it.

So it's provocative, she thought defiantly. But it's my show—mine and Holly's—and people expect artists to dress so that they stand out from the crowd, don't they?

White choker beads and matching earrings hanging low added a finishing touch to the outfit.

Casey jumped back in exaggerated surprise when he called to pick her up.

'Dressed to kill,' he commented as they drove to the gallery. 'But who? The tenant?'

'He's not here. He's away.' Lauren tried to keep the dull note from her voice.

'Alone? Or with the lady-friend?' He thought a moment, brain clearly busy with an interesting idea. 'Or abroad, perhaps, revisiting the scene of his abduction?'

Lauren frowned. 'With a view to what?'

'Writing about it, maybe?'

She hoped she had kept her face expressionless. 'Don't be silly. Who would revisit a place where they'd been through such a terrible ordeal?' Casey Talbert was a darned sight too fast-thinking, she reflected. But that was a vital asset, wasn't it, in his kind of job?

Holly had arrived before them. Her outfit—black sweater, white trousers—also caught Casey's eye, and he whistled appreciatively.

'If the sweater fits, as they used to say when women

were women and proud of it, get a size smaller.' He made curving gestures through the air. 'And is Holly Dixon's sweater a size smaller.'

Holly, pink-cheeked, laughed, clearly pleased with Casey's reaction.

'Lauren, isn't this just great?' She touched Casey's arm and he looked at her hand as though he liked the gesture. 'Thanks a lot, Casey, for making it all possible.'

He made a sweeping bow, then commented, 'Hey, it hasn't started yet. Shouldn't you keep your thanks until we see what happens? Maybe no one will come.'

As if to prove him wrong, the first visitors came up the stairs. They were, they said, too eager even to wait for the official opening. They just had to look around straight away.

From that moment, the two girls hardly had a minute to themselves. Harry Harper, editor of the newspaper for which Casey worked, was due at any moment to perform the opening ceremony.

'Miss Halstead?'

Lauren turned to find a grey-haired man addressing her. 'I am,' she said, and with a smile she added, taking a guess, 'Mr Hartingford?'

He extended a hand. 'Happy to meet you, Miss Halstead. You remember our phone conversation?'

'About the book you're going to write about birds? Of course I do.'

'I've been looking round. May I congratulate you on your ability? Some of your landscapes, I have to say it, are inspired.'

Lauren coloured a little, remembering the circumstances which had brought them into being. Brett had spent the night with his lady-friend—which, she thought, gazing round with dull eyes, he had probably been doing each night since he had left the house two days ago.

'Thank you for saying so, Mr Hartingford. I'm looking forward to starting the project—'

'Which won't be for a while, I'm afraid. I have to take a trip to New Zealand to see my sister. She's a little older than I am, and she hasn't been too well lately. But I shall certainly contact you again on my return.'

The crowd was quietening down, and Edward Hartingford, noticing that the opening ceremony was about to take place, stood back. Casey's editor had happily agreed to perform it, and his few words of welcome and praise for the two young artists who had provided such an excellent display of talent were greeted with applause.

Casey's uncle took Lauren's hand, putting an avuncular arm around Holly's shoulders. 'I'm proud of you both,' he commented, then added, 'The buffet—' he indicated the tables, the food they bore being temporarily covered '—will be open soon.'

There was a slight disturbance at the top of the stairs which led directly into the gallery. Lauren's head swung round. All the evening she had been hoping for the appearance of the one man in the world she longed to see. It was no use telling herself that he had never promised to be there. All the same, disappointment had gripped her every time she had searched for him in vain.

Now at last he was here, and Lauren could hardly believe her eyes. Then she saw that he was not alone.

CHAPTER TEN

How could she not have expected it? she reproached herself. With Imogen Gard in town he would never go anywhere alone, would he? Not even to bed... Even so, her eyes locked with his, until she tore hers away, only to feel them drawn to him again.

He was looking at her as though he had never seen her before, looking her over as if they'd never met, as if she had never shared a bed with him, made love with him... She wanted to scrunch up her programme and throw it at him, anything to take that sensual look from his eyes, and that mouth that was so cynically twisted, as if he were categorising her as a soft touch, always willing...

So she was dressed sexily, perhaps even—for her—a little outrageously, but surely he of all people knew that she wasn't really a seductive tease, that she wasn't an easy target for just any man?

Imogen moved forward, seemingly attracted by Casey, who stared at her as if he couldn't take his eyes away. If Imogen Gard was that attractive to a man in his twenties, Lauren agonised, how much more magnetic must she be to someone as sophisticated and worldly as Brett?

'Hi,' Casey said to Imogen. 'You want a guide to show you round?'

Imogen inclined her head, her smile synthetically sweet. Casey needed no further encouragement and led the woman to the tiered display of Holly's work, leaving Brett standing alone.

Lauren found herself moving towards him. 'Thank you for coming after all,' she offered with a tremulous smile. 'I'd almost given up—'

'Brett Carmichael?' A man had moved faster, reaching Brett's side first. 'Harry Harper—editor, *News Journal*. Haven't I heard of you somewhere? You're Australian? Don't you belong down under?'

'Hi,' said Brett, changing in a flash from predatory male to professional journalist. Their hands met briefly. 'British, born and bred.'

Harry shook his head. 'Can't believe it. I've seen you somewhere... I've got it! I was on a long visit to relatives in Queensland a few years ago. On the telly. That's where I saw you. Reporting news from all over the southern hemisphere. Right?'

'Right,' Brett said. 'I'm not based there now. It's a long story.'

'Be glad to hear it some time over a drink. Hey, Casey—' he turned, tapped his wristwatch '—got a minute? I'll have to go.'

With reluctance, Casey took his leave of Imogen, whose attention was seized by an eager Holly, who had noticed that the woman held one of her models.

'Brett.' It was all Lauren could manage. 'You've been away a—' A long time? It would be stupid to let him know how much she'd missed him. With a companion like Imogen, how could he have missed her, Lauren? she asked herself with a twist of pain.

'Yes, I've been away. Where have you been?' She knew what he meant by the way his eyes seemed to strip her naked. 'Where's the girl I left behind?'

Lauren's cheeks grew hot. 'I don't know what you mean—unless you're implying—'

'Yeah. That louse Casey...and you. How else could you be looking so...?' Again his eyes disparaged her.

'Shameless?' Lauren held up her head. 'Thanks for your belief in my integrity. And so what if I am dressed like this?' She pointed to the gaping fastening of her fitted top and the daring slit in her skirt, then wished she hadn't because his eyes dropped to those parts of her anatomy. 'It's what the public expect of an artist, isn't it?'

Eyebrows arched. 'Is it?'

'Yes. And if we're in the business of insults about our respective private lives, how about you and—?'

He straightened to his full height from the stone pillar against which he had been leaning. He had meant to intimidate, Lauren knew that, and he had succeeded. In all the circumstances, he had effectively silenced her.

Imogen approached, holding a filled plate in one hand and in the other a package which clearly contained one of Holly's models. 'We aren't leaving yet, are we, darling?' she asked, throwing a 'he's mine' smile at Lauren.

'Miss Halstead?' One of the women visitors caught Lauren's attention. 'There's a painting of yours I'd love to buy. Could you price it for me, please?'

As Lauren dealt with the delighted customer she noticed out of the corner of her eye that Brett was alone again, a plate of food in one hand and a glass in the other. Now and then he paused in front of one of her paintings, then passed on. . .and on.

Pushing the signed cheque she had received into her pocket, Lauren could not prevent her feet from taking her to his side.

'Brett?'

'Mmm?' It seemed he knew her identity without needing to turn his head.

'What—what do you think of it—them—my work?'

'I've told you before, it's good.' He paused. 'These landscapes—they're brooding. There's a hidden darkness about them, like a storm brewing.' His head turned and there was a gleam in his eyes. 'In the elements themselves or—' he paused again '—in your mind?'

His penetrating perception bowled her over. 'I—my mind was in something of a turmoil,' she conceded reluctantly.

'Oh? Why?'

How could she tell him the reason, that he had been the cause, with his apparent close relationship with his father's ex-wife?

'On the other hand—' she dodged the question '—it did begin to rain after that, and I had to dash for cover.'

He looked her over. 'I remember. You arrived home looking like a drowned—'

'Don't you dare say "rat",' Lauren broke in. Their smiles mingled and her heart hit a high note.

'OK.' He put aside his empty plate and glass and pretended to think. 'Cat, then. Any better?'

'Not really. Unless—unless you mean by that something you can stroke.' She knew she was being provocative, but she had ceased caring.

His narrowed glance raked her, and again it lingered on her burgeoning breasts, the outline of which could be traced through the thin material of her top as the button opening gaped. He only had to be near her, she realised with a touch of dismay, for her body to react to him, giving him 'come on' signs as if vital areas of her anatomy had minds of their own.

'Oh, yes, I'd stroke that particular cat.' His gaze searched for and found Casey Talbert. 'Wouldn't anybody—any male man?'

'If you're implying that I'd allow any man—'

'Forget it,' came sharply back at her.

There was a breath-holding pause, then she said, 'Brett?' His gaze lifted reluctantly from her body to fix intently on her grey eyes. She gestured towards her paintings. 'Do you really think I've got enough—well, talent to get some kind of recognition one day? That is, if I try hard enough?'

'Still fishing for compliments?'

His evasive and taunting answer hurt, and she turned away.

'Lauren—' His hand closed round her wrist, pulling her back.

She would never know what he had been going to say. Imogen, eyes on their connecting hands, swept over and touched his shoulder, running her palm down his chest to his waist.

Lauren pulled free and aimlessly wandered off, not wishing to hear the exchange of intimate trivialities which she was sure would follow.

Casey was again in conversation with his boss, Lauren noticed as she walked around. Their backs were to the crowd and their profiles seemed to hold a kind of furtiveness that worried her—as if there was a conspiracy between them, against. . .what, whom?

Harry Harper gestured now and then, seeming to point down at the floor and then indicate the room behind him, milling with guests. Lauren could not tell for sure, and a strange unease gripped her—especially when she saw Casey peer carefully over his shoulder, only to meet her eyes and withdraw his quickly.

It was only after she had completed the sale of another painting and shaken hands with the happy purchaser that Lauren had a chance to look around again, but Brett—and Imogen—had gone.

Casey drove Lauren home, and it took her only seconds to discover that Brett was not there either. But he and Imogen had called there, judging by the two used coffee-cups on top of the dishwasher.

After the bustle and chatter of the exhibition, the house was unbearably silent. Even Casey seemed to feel it as he entered the kitchen behind Lauren. He stood still, listening like a creature after prey.

'Not here?' he asked.

'How did you guess?'

'Hey, why so sour after all I've done for you?'

Lauren forced her mood to change. Smiling, she put a hand on Casey's arm.

'Sorry. And thanks a lot for everything.' She clasped her hands. 'I never dreamt I'd sell so many pictures.'

She counted on her fingers. 'Would you believe—seven? In one evening!'

'If you go on like that, you'll run out of supplies before the show's over. Holly did well too, she said.'

'I can't thank your uncle enough, Casey. Like a coffee?'

In the kitchen he spied the empty cups. 'Seems like someone's beaten you to it. Now, I wonder who?' He leant against the kitchen units, arms folded, eyes roaming. 'Lauren, what's between those two?'

'You mean Brett and his—' She stopped herself abruptly. She'd almost called Imogen his ex-stepmother.

Casey noticed the hesitation and his head swung round.

'His lady-friend?' Lauren continued hastily. 'What could there possibly be? I mean, she's twelve years older than he is—'

'How do you know? So precisely, I mean?'

She'd slipped up there! 'Guesswork,' she declared with bravado. 'How else? I mean, she *looks*—' She frowned. 'What is this, Casey? An interrogation?'

'Sorry.' He gestured. 'Kettle's boiling.' He wandered round, picking up and putting down recipe books, leafing through the weekend magazines which were in a pile on a side table, flicking over the letter rack.

'Nothing there addressed to the chief investigative reporter of *News Journal*,' Lauren commented, pretending to joke.

'In other words, keep off.' Casey thrust his hands into his pockets. 'Sorry.' He tapped his nose. 'Always on the scent, this bit of me.'

'You won't find anything to interest you here.'

'No?'

'No. Not in this room. Who leaves exciting clues—not that there are any in this house—in a kitchen?'

They drank their coffee in the living room, and afterwards Casey roamed restlessly again.

He pulled books from the low shelves, opened them, flicked through their pages and replaced them, then swung round.

'What do you say, Lauren, to an end-of-show party tomorrow?'

'But Casey, I couldn't expect your uncle to—'

'Not at the gallery. Here, in this room.' He half closed his eyes reminiscently. 'Remember Marie's party, before she and Reggie drove off into the night without warning?'

'Only too clearly,' Lauren answered. 'When you got so drunk you followed me around like a devoted pet.'

He smiled ruefully.

And when the man I've grown to love so much came out of the shadows and fainted at my feet, she added silently.

'A party would be fine by me,' she said aloud, 'as long as it's a bring-your-own.'

'Bottles and grub—OK, I'll contact the gang.'

The telephone pealed into the short silence. Lauren put down her mug and made a dive for it. At this hour it just had to be Brett.

'Lauren Halstead? Good. Glad you're not in bed yet. This is Harry Harper, *News Journal* editor.'

'Hi, Mr Harper.' Lauren hoped she had managed to disguise her disappointment. 'How may I help you?'

'Since I got home I've been thinking. You're a great little artist, Miss Halstead, and I thought it might give your future prospects a boost if we ran a couple of articles about you in the magazine we include with the paper each month. Photographs of you, your studio and so on. A bit about your lifestyle—you get it?'

Lauren felt a glow of pleasure. Maybe this meant she was on the brink of recognition in the world of art!

'A few questions to start with, Miss Halstead. The house you're living in—Old Cedar Grange, yes? It's not your home, is it? But the name of the true owner escapes me. . .'

'Gard,' Lauren readily supplied. 'Mr Redmund Gard.'

'Ah, yes. And he's left you in charge, while he...?' The pause implied a question to be answered.

'Lives abroad. He's out of touch at present,' Lauren informed her questioner. 'Wandering the world, as he called it.'

'He's due back—when?'

'No idea, Mr Harper.'

'In the meantime you continue to live there?'

'Looking after the house, yes.'

'May I ask, Miss Halstead—alone?'

Confused, Lauren hesitated, then, remembering that she was talking to a powerful member of the newspaper's journalistic team, she decided to prevaricate. 'Well, Casey's with me at the moment.'

'Ah, yes. Good. I'll be in touch, Miss Halstead.' The call was over.

Lauren found Casey upstairs in her studio. She had had a vague sense of him wandering about while she was on the phone, and wondered where he had got to. He was pushing a small notebook into his pocket as she entered.

'Just imagine!' she exclaimed, sinking down onto her canvas stool. 'I've been interviewed, prior to being interviewed.' She laughed happily. 'By guess who? Your *editor*. He didn't put a junior onto the story!'

Casey's smile was a little twisted. 'There's fame for you. The editor, not me—Casey Talbert.'

'Photographs too, to go with the words. Jealous?' she teased him.

'Not a bit. You deserve it. Er—how much of your work did you manage to sell this evening? I've been trying to remember.'

Hence the notebook, she guessed. As she had disposed of her paintings she had asked him to make a note of their titles. She counted on her fingers once more and he drew out the notebook again, turning the page and writing down the total.

His restlessness seemed to have left him, and he pulled Lauren up from the stool and swung her round. 'You know, in that gear tonight, I could have eaten you. I noticed Carmichael giving you the eye half a dozen times. Come on, Lauren—' his hold on her arm tightened, and she didn't like it at all '—give.'

Oh God, she thought, is it true I look like a woman who'd say yes to every man? Brett seemed to think so too.

She pushed Casey to arm's length. 'You want a kiss?'

'More than that.'

'One kiss.' She turned her cheek, but he found her mouth. His kiss was unrefined and, against Brett's, totally ineffective. She forced herself to smile, managing to evade his groping hands. 'Sorry, Casey. I've said my thanks. Thanks again for everything. That's it. Goodnight.'

'OK, I'm a guy who knows when to stop. Then I can try another time, can't I?'

When he had gone, Lauren felt the silence wrap around her. She wandered about the kitchen, tidying, straightening. When she came to the letter rack on one of the cupboards, she tidied the contents of that too.

As she brought some order to the envelopes which sloped this way and that she noticed a few slips of paper bearing Brett's handwriting. They seemed to be brief notes he had made for the book he was writing.

Either he'd pushed them in absentmindedly or had put them there on his way to an appointment, telling himself he would know where to find them when he needed them. Deciding to leave them there, she made her way to the living room and stood staring out of the window.

The cedar tree stood enigmatically, its moonlit branches splashing arm-like shadows across the walls and windows of the house. In her tiredness she thought she saw Brett's outline. He's here, she thought, heart-beats speeding, ready to thrust open the doors and run to him. Oh, yes, she thought, he's come back... But when she looked again, she knew that her imagination had been playing tricks.

The clamour was increasing, the chatter competing with the hi-fi for a hearing. Marie's friends had come at Casey's bidding, all 'paying their respects', as one of them put it, to Lauren and Holly's art show.

Earlier that day Casey had helped Lauren and Holly to pack their pictures and modelled figures. First he had delivered Holly's boxes to her house, then he had taken her on, with Lauren and her paintings, to Old Cedar Grange.

Now the party was in full swing, much of the food having been brought, courtesy of Casey's uncle, in a special van from Chez Talbert to the house.

When Lauren had offered to pay, Henry Talbert had dismissed the gesture.

'You and Holly, not to mention my dear nephew, have brought so many extra clients to my restaurant I can hardly thank *you* enough, my dear,' he'd said.

Casey was dancing with Holly, Lauren with Johnny—the young man who, on the night of Marie and Reggie's party, had helped to convey Brett, in his semi-collapsed state, up the stairs.

'You didn't, did you?' Johnny asked Lauren.

'Didn't what? Oh. Fall for my tenant, you mean?' She glanced away, smiled. 'It's a landlady's strictest rule—never get romantic ideas about male lodgers. Didn't you know?'

'That's no answer,' Johnny said, swinging her round and back, just as Casey was doing with Holly.

'It's the only answer you're going to get,' Lauren retorted.

There was a squeal from a young woman near the

patio doors, which had been flung open to let in the cool midnight air.

'There's a man in the garden. He might be a—a criminal!'

Oh, no, Lauren thought, breaking away from her partner. Not again—not another gatecrasher... She glanced outside and instant recognition jolted the breath from her body.

That man belongs to the house—but most of all, she wanted to cry out, he belongs to me. Her legs, taking her through the doors, could not move fast enough for her liking.

He lounged against the cedar tree, arms folded. She halted in front of him. There was no backpack on the ground this time, no stubble round an unshaven jaw.

He wore a suit, and beside him, where he had dropped it, was a black executive case. His hair was neatly combed, his shirt a startling white in the semi-darkness.

'Brett?' she whispered hoarsely. 'You're back?'

'Who else were you expecting?' came drily from him.

'Who is it?' It was Casey's voice. 'If he's threatening you—'

Oh, yes, he's threatening me, Lauren thought, but not in the way you mean. My heart, my body and my soul, the rest of my life...

'It's OK, Casey, Brett's come back—Brett Carmichael.' In her excitement, her voice had hit a high note.

There was a groan from Casey. 'Heck, it's *him*?'

'Brett—' Lauren gestured towards the glass-paned doors '—join us.' He did not move. 'Come to the party. *Please*. It's a celebration.' She moved closer, lifting her face, full of appeal. Their eyes locked. 'Holly and I have sold so much of our work, we just had to let off steam somehow.' She extended her hand. 'Brett? Will you come and dance? Brett?' There was an unintentional wobble in her voice, which told him she was pleading, but she didn't care.

It seemed to take him time to react. His eyes scanned the guests who, losing interest, were retreating.

Slowly Brett straightened, taking her hand and moving into the crowd. Someone had turned up the music again and the dancing was resumed, more romantic now, the pace slower.

Brett held out his arms and Lauren went into them, closing her eyes, her emotions lifting her to a high she had reached only once before—and that had been in those same arms.

Someone nudged her shoulder. 'I've got my answer,' muttered Johnny out of the side of his mouth. 'You've been a fool, Lauren. I did warn you.' And with his partner, he moved away.

'You've missed me?' Brett asked, voice low.

'What do you think?' Their eyes held, their limbs doing their own thing—his hard as they brushed against her, hers melting so much that she had to rely on his hold for support. 'Have you missed *me*? No, don't answer that. Of course you haven't. You haven't been alone, have you?'

'I won't answer that either.'

'The food's all gone,' someone shouted.

'And the bottles are empty.' Somebody else took up the theme.

'Get them out, Lauren,' Brett said against her ear. 'I want you.'

Her head jerked back, eyes accusing. 'You can say that, when you've as good as admitted your lady-friend has been with you?'

'I did no such thing. Get them out,' he repeated sharply.

'But she was, wasn't she?' Lauren persisted, wanting—yet not wanting—to know the truth.

'If she was, it was not in the way you're insinuating.'

Her heart tripped. So Imogen *had* been with him—

probably all the time he'd been away. It was she, Lauren, who wanted the party over now. What had she to celebrate any more, knowing the truth at last?

Breaking away, she announced, 'Party's over everybody.' Forcing a smile, she spread her arms. 'Thanks for all your support.'

Brett propped himself against the wall, hands in pockets, watching the room empty. Soon only Casey and Holly were left, and Holly had gone to the cloakroom to collect her jacket.

Casey slipped outside through the opened doors by the garden, and returned holding Brett's case, arm stretched towards him.

'You wouldn't want a thief to steal all your secrets, Mr Carmichael, now would you?' he asked with a false lightness of tone.

Brett inclined his head, accepting his executive case and dropping it onto a chair, and Casey went to stand beside Lauren—at which Brett's arm shot out, pulling her to his side.

'You've got treasure there,' commented Casey, eyes first on the case, then sliding to rest on Lauren.

'Gold bars, maybe?' Lauren joked, trying to lighten the taut atmosphere.

'Yeah, gold, Mr Talbert,' Brett shot back. 'Gold of the purest kind. Not a smear of dross in sight.'

Teeth were snapping—metaphorically, of course. In her thoughts, Lauren imagined the two men circling each other. Who would spring first? Who would vanquish whom?

It was Casey who weakened, his gaze dropping, conceding victory, but it was his thrust-out jaw that worried Lauren.

'Thanks again, Casey,' she put in quickly, 'for all your help and your uncle's—'

Her hand was seized and she found herself in Casey's arms, his lips forcing a kiss from hers. To keep her balance, she had to hold onto his shoulders.

'Thanks, sweetheart,' he said in a falsely silky tone, 'for all *your* help—for your co-operation and collaboration.'

'No, no,' she got out, more than a little puzzled, 'I'm the one who should be thanking *you* for all that.'

'You think?' Casey responded, to her complete incomprehension.

Brett pulled her back to his side. 'Get out, Talbert. It's impolite to keep a lady waiting.' He gestured towards Holly, who was watching the proceedings from the doorway, a frown on her gentle face.

Lauren tensed apprehensively at Casey's expression. It was not so much a grin as an unpleasant drawing back of lips over teeth. And it was directed at her.

Head down, eyes closed, Lauren did not stir until the sound of Casey's car drawing away told her everyone had gone.

Then, half-heartedly, she moved to tidy the after-party chaos.

'Leave it,' Brett ordered.

'How can I? Otherwise, it'll all be here in the morning—'

'Leave it, I said. And come here.'

Lauren looked at him, not liking the set of his jaw, the hard glint in his eyes. 'Why should I—?'

Again he seized her, standing her in front of him.

'You enjoyed that clinch, did you, *sweetheart*?' he grated, mocking Casey's use of the endearment. 'You liked being in Talbert's arms?'

She watched him drawing a clean, folded handkerchief from his pocket.

'Of course not. If you thought I was holding onto him out of *love* for him, you couldn't be more wrong. I'd have fallen if I hadn't—'

The handkerchief, drawn roughly backwards and forwards across her mouth, cut off her protests.

'Those lips are mine to do as I like with.' The words came through Brett's teeth. 'Not one centimetre of them belongs to that bastard.' He dropped the hand-kerchief as if it were too sullied to be used again.

'I said—' he pulled her against him '—I want you. I want you, Lauren.' His voice had roughened. 'My God, you don't know how much.'

She ran her tongue over her dry lips. 'Brett, I—'

'Shut up.' His arms tugged her closer and his mouth took over hers. She felt the hardness of his need pressing into the yielding softness of her flesh. Her body's desire for his total possession grew unbearably.

'Right time, wrong place,' he mouthed against her lips and scooped her up, striding two at a time up the stairs.

His bed had been roughly made and he stood her down beside it. 'This outfit you're wearing,' he said thickly, 'has been driving me crazy since I first saw you in it. These buttons—' one by one he pulled them apart '—were made for male fingers to undo.' He began at the hem, working his way up. With two to go, he paused, placing a searing kiss on her mouth. His hand invaded, spread wide, found her breasts. 'As I guessed, no bra. I've been wondering; now I know.'

Then the remaining two buttons popped open and he bent his head, winding his tongue around the hardened flesh, suckling, nipping until she cried out her pleasure.

His other hand had not been idle, finding the long slit in her skirt and cupping the curve of her rear, his nails bringing little chokes of pain and enjoyment. She gasped at the mixture of gentleness and cruelty, her eyes closing, her mind whirling in rotations of ecstasy and exquisite agony.

She was naked now, and he threw her onto the bed. Her heart pounded with arousal and anticipation as she watched him bare his muscled body and display the full extent of his manhood. I can do that to him? she thought in hazy wonder. He wants me that much?

All over again he began his arousal, stroking her

stomach, her inner thighs, finding places so intimate she could hardly contain her twisting, writhing need of him.

'Now, oh, now, darling,' she cried out. 'Don't keep me waiting any longer...'

His low laugh was intended to torment as he delayed his thrust of possession, and tormented she was—reaching out for him, offering herself, all of her body and all of her soul.

At last he entered her, the rhythm of his need beginning slowly, then speeding ever faster, taking her with him to the very heights of pleasure and fulfilment.

It was late next morning when she rolled back into his arms, stroking his hair, placing small kisses over his jaw, even though he was not fully awake.

I love you, Brett Carmichael, she wanted to whisper. I know love doesn't mean anything to you, because if it did you would never have deserted your daughter and the mother of your child. Nor, in the first place, would you have had an affair with the woman who was, after all, your stepmother. Oh, God, she thought—*his father's wife.*

She began to ease away, wriggling towards the edge of the bed. He stirred, dragging her back. 'What's wrong?'

She shook her head and her body remained stiff and resistant to his stroking hand. His fingers around her jaw forced her to look at him. 'Out with it, Lauren.'

She knew, in the circumstances, that he would not tolerate prevarication—which meant she had no option but to tell him.

'You've got a daughter. Remember? You've got responsibilities where she's concerned. Not to mention your—your daughter's mother.'

He stroked her hair, keeping her body against his. 'Would you believe me if I told you that Elissa is not my daughter? That I have no progeny? Don't you know me well enough now to accept that I wouldn't refuse to acknowledge the existence of my offspring if I had any?'

She had to keep probing to get at the truth. 'But that letter I found in that book—the one your father wrote to you—'

'He was wrong, Lauren. Whoever fathered that child we may never know, but it was not me.'

'But Brett—her name—Elissa—Ellis—she was named for you.'

'So?'

She wanted so much to believe him, to believe that the stories his father had allowed to be published about him were not true, but she pressed on. 'You had affairs—lots of them.'

He listened, expressionless, his arms still round her, but loosened now. Was she losing him? Were her accusations cutting a chasm between them that she would never again be able to cross, keeping him away from her forever. 'W-worst of all—' she forced herself to go on '—you had an affair with your father's second wife...your *stepmother*.'

For a few terrible moments he did not speak.

'So it's true, your stepmother was your lover?' Could her heart sink any lower?'

'My stepmother had a lover. I was not that lover.' He spoke quietly, decisively.

'Oh, darling.' She clung to him, hiding her face against his chest. 'I want to believe you.'

He lifted her chin, looking intently into her eyes, almost as though he were drinking from them. 'I've said this before, Lauren, and I'm saying it again. You have to trust me until—'

'Until when, Brett?' she whispered, her fingers lightly touching his mouth.

'For God's sake, Lauren. This is what matters.'

His arms tightened around her and he swung her above him.

She felt his instant arousal and was glad, because the love she felt for him overcame all moral arguments. The lines of her body softened as she submitted again, opening out to him, doing as he wanted, more than ever needing him inside her, possessing her utterly.

Afterwards she nestled into him, and his arms closed around her, pulling her against him. Soon, as he took her again—and, not so much later, yet again—Lauren thought that life could hold no geater happiness and that paradise itself was within her grasp.

Except that if she dared to reach out for it, it would slip away, she was certain. If only. . .if only the past—his past—had never been.

CHAPTER ELEVEN

IT WAS lunchtime before they made any real effort to start the working day. Their meal was leisurely and light—neither, each confessed, feeling the need for food, their appetites having been satisfied, as Lauren so poetically put it, much to Brett's amusement, by the food of love.

While Brett returned to his office to continue with his writing, Lauren worked in the studio on commissions from customers who had seen the word 'sold' on her paintings and requested her to produce copies especially for them.

When they met in the kitchen for an afternoon cup of tea, Brett pulled Lauren onto his lap while they drank. There was suddenly a sound at the front door as if something had been delivered, and they looked at each other, frowning.

'Did you order an evening newspaper?' Lauren asked, at which Brett shook his head.

'You?' he queried, and as Lauren shook her head too, they laughed and kissed—Brett only reluctantly allowing her to leave him, holding her hand until she was too far away to reach, then making her promise to come back.

'Just try and stop me,' she said.

She was gone so long he went in search of her, calling her name. He discovered her in the entrance hall, with the afternoon edition of the *News Journal* opened wide.

'What's wrong?' he asked indulgently. 'Your show had a bad write-up from the art correspondent?'

She lowered the newspaper, staring at him, her face paper-white, the news-sheet shaking in her trembling hands.

He frowned, taking the journal. 'What's wrong?' he repeated. 'Somebody you know died?'

You could say that, she thought, running her tongue over parched lips. He came to look over her shoulder. Unable, now, to hide any of its contents, she handed the newspaper over.

As Brett read Lauren felt the need of the wall's support. She closed her eyes, barely able to breathe.

She was waiting for the onslaught, the verbal avalanche, the accusations and condemnations. Yet she wasn't guilty; she was as innocent of the miserable, low-down deed as a newborn baby.

When it came, she could hardly bear it. Brett closed the pages, shutting in the photograph of his modelled head on its column in the garden, and, below it, the picture of the two damaged paintings, which, Lauren was absolutely certain, had been shut away again in the secret room next to the library.

The blood had drained from his cheeks too. Worse, the stare he turned on her was like a Hallowe'en mask—but more threatening, more frightening.

'Who gave that swine this private information? You?'

She nearly choked. 'Me? You can't believe that. You as good as swore me to silence about the book you're writing. I've kept that promise. And I've never, *never* told Casey anything—anything at all about your real identity, or about what your father did when he sent you away from him.'

His teeth snapped and he bundled the paper onto a hall chair. 'That kind of information,' he said grimly, raking in a pocket and producing his car keys, 'would be in the *News Journal* library—in the back numbers, or in the cuttings library.' He swung to face her again. 'But it would have to be someone in the know to put that louse onto this story.'

The look in his eyes made her want to faint. 'Not me, Brett. You *must* believe me. Don't stare at me like that.' She shook her head violently, then used attack as defence. 'If you don't believe me on this, how can you ask me to believe you about your past? Why should I not accept that all your father said about you in that letter was the truth?'

'Because it was wrong. From start to finish it was wrong.'

'So are you about this, Brett. So are you!' Her voice had risen in her desire to convince him of her innocence.

He walked out and slammed the door behind him, but Lauren opened it again, calling out as he got into his car, 'Where are you going?' But her words were drowned by the roar of the engine.

She closed the door and leaned against it, head back, utterly dejected. What meaning was there now in the intimacies they'd shared only hours—or was it years—ago?

As she reached for the newspaper the phone rang.

'Did you get the *Journal*?' Casey asked.

'So *you* sent it?'

'Who else? Did you like the feature I did? Did you-know-who see it?'

'He did. You cost me dear, Casey Talbert. You cost me—' My life's happiness. . .she wanted to say. 'Who gave you all that information? I kept my promise to Brett. I didn't breathe a word about his private life, nor his writing activities.'

'You underrated the journalistic mind, Lauren. There's such a thing as putting two and two together, making connections, using your instincts, your intelligence. Any good journalist will tell you that. Add to that the fact that I had the run of the house—'

'When?'

'That phone call after the opening?'

'When your editor interviewed me about the art show?'

'You're dead right—hey, what the hell's happening across the room? Who the heck let *him* in?'

The clatter told her that the phone had dropped to his desk-top. He sounded terrified.

'Where's Talbert?' a voice rang out. 'Where's his desk?' The voice, so dear, so familiar, yet at that moment so harsh and frightening, sounded loudly in Lauren's ear.

'H-hi there, Brett. Good to see you, old friend.' Casey's tone was placatory, but to no avail.

'I have something to say to you, *friend*.' The tone was menacing. 'Where do you want me to say it? Here or outside?'

'It's the great Brett Carmichael, isn't it?' queried one of the other journalists in the background. 'Guys, we have a television personality in our midst.'

'Somebody got a pair of pistols?' joked a colleague. 'Some duel this is going to be.'

'No joking. That guy means it.'

'Which cesspool did you dig that story out of, Talbert? Who put you onto it?'

'But Mr Carmichael, I was only doing my job. Ask my editor, Harry Harper. He recognised you at the art show, remember? He said you were worth a story and to get something on you.'

'Tell me,' Brett was saying through his teeth, 'who told you. If you don't I'll sue you for libel until you have to go begging to live.'

'M-my sources, Brett. Got to protect them. You should know that. Hey, wait a minute, Brett—'

There was the sound of a scuffle.

'Keep them apart!' The warning shout was genuine now.

Lauren cried, 'No, Brett, no. Don't hurt him. For heaven's sake—for your sake—'

The phone at the other end was grasped. 'Don't you mean for *your* sake? He means that much to you?'

'No, Brett, you've got it wrong.'

'I could've told you that it was over a woman,' a cynical reporter's voice was saying. 'Always is.'

'OK, OK, I'll tell you. But you won't like it,' Casey said. 'It was her—Lauren.'

She opened her mouth to shout her innocence, but the receiver at the other end clattered onto its cradle.

The meaning behind Casey's curious gratitude last night for her 'help, co-operation and collaboration' hit her like a bullet. He had known what was coming, that he intended to involve her in his deceitful act—had known full well that it would end her relationship with Brett as swiftly as a sword slashing through the air.

Shaken to the point of collapse by all she had heard, Lauren retrieved the crumpled newspaper, carrying it into the kitchen. Their half-empty coffee-mugs, hers and Brett's, stood side by side.

And that, she agonised, was about the nearest they would ever be together again. The entire world had changed in the twenty minutes since she had left Brett's lap to collect from the doorstep the *News Journal*— which she had never ordered anyway.

With slow, hopeless movements, she spread the newspaper over the wooden table and started to read Casey's report. Its heading shouted: LOCAL BOY MAKES IT BIG DOWN UNDER, and in smaller print it went on, MAN WITH TWO NAMES. Lauren read on.

> Do the inhabitants of this town realise that they have a celebrity living among them? He is none other than Brett Carmichael, well-known Australian TV journalist and one-time owner of his own news agency.
>
> Did you also know, folks, that this man is also Ellis Gard, the prodigal son of Redmund Gard, one-time resident of this town? Father and son have neither met nor corresponded for at least fifteen years. And why? Because son took stepmother away from his own father. And it's whispered, dear readers, that—

Oh, God, Lauren thought, taking a few sips of water from a glass which shook in her trembling hand, he surely hasn't printed that story? But he had.

—that the offspring of the liaison was a lovely daughter. She's in her teens now, and still at school, so she shall be nameless.

Want to know more? There's another secret about this man from the shadows. He's writing a book about his experiences—and what experiences. For nearly two years he lived a life of hell after he was taken hostage by jungle rebels. You'll have to buy the book to find out more.

Eyes closed, Lauren held her head. How could Casey make such legally questionable statements? Hadn't his editor warned him? Then she remembered the editor's phone call. Where was his report about the art show? In her anguish she squeezed handfuls of the newsprint, combing the paper from front to back and to the front page again. She could find not a single word about it.

She dragged herself to the living room and collapsed into an armchair. As Casey had been about to tell her when Brett had appeared in the newspaper office, she, Lauren, had been set up, had taken the bait and swallowed it whole.

She recalled the editor's body language as he'd talked to Casey at the art show, his finger jabbing downwards, as if indicating the southern hemisphere, and then to the guests behind him, implying, as she now knew, that he was talking about one guest in particular.

He had heard from Casey that he was taking Lauren home, and that had been the moment when the phone call had been arranged between them. Lauren's attention, it must have been decided, would temporarily be distracted, giving Casey time to wander unhindered round the house. He would search for clues, for anything he could find about Brett Carmichael.

Although how could he have discovered a single clue as to Brett's writing activities? When Casey had gone, had she found anything out of place? The letter rack! She had blamed Brett for its untidiness, but she now realised that would have been foreign to his meticulous nature.

She ran to the kitchen. The rack stood there, as she had expected, tidy and neat. The small sheets of notes belonging to Brett which she had discovered amongst the envelopes were not there now. But they'd been there then; she knew that for certain.

The doorbell rang as if someone was leaning on it. Only Casey demanded entry in that way.

'Where's that big-headed swine? Is he back yet?' He smoothed down his hair. 'Thought by now I'd have to tear you from his murderous arms.'

'He hasn't arrived yet,' Lauren snapped. 'How can you possibly call him big-headed?'

'Thinks he's God's gift to women just because he was a cult TV personality down under.'

'He really was?'

'Yeah. Didn't he ever tell you?'

'No. And stop trying to distract me, Casey Talbert. You dropped me right in it. You lied. I heard you.'

'Lauren, I just did my homework. I went to the *Journal*'s library and turned to the back numbers. I found Redmund Gard's vindictive report of fifteen years ago about his son's alleged amorous activities. But the bit about you helping me was true, Lauren— well, partly.'

'I'm glad you qualified that statement.' She took him up sharply. 'All *I* told you was that Brett was working in his room. Then you, with your nasty, unscrupulous mind, filled in the gaps, building on the very few hints I might have dropped accidentally.' She added thoughtfully, 'Which means you didn't give away your sources after all.' Turning on her sweetest smile, she went close to him, 'Who were they, Casey, those "sources" of yours?'

He looked down at her fingers playing with a lapel on his jacket.

'What's this?' His eyes held an anticipatory gleam. 'What're you trying to tell me, Lauren, sweetie? That you care after all?' His hand moved to rest on her waist, drawing her closer.

'You answer my question first, then I might answer yours.'

She knew she was being provocative, and felt uncomfortable in the role, but his answer was so important that she had deliberately put aside her scruples to get it.

The front door burst open and Brett stood there. His gaze, fixing on the close proximity of their bodies, clearly misinterpreted it.

'So—' Brett's eyes narrowed '—you two really are in collusion—in more ways than one.'

Casey made a dive for the door, sliding past Brett as if he were afraid he might spring and tear him apart.

'Cheers, Lauren,' he said, then, looking from her to Brett, he added, 'Good luck, pal. Sooner you than me.'

With a quick wave, he put the door between them.

'We're not, Brett,' Lauren said defensively. 'In collusion, I mean. You were here when the newspaper arrived. You saw for yourself how horrified I was to read what Casey had written.'

'Just because you didn't know the contents in advance, that doesn't mean you didn't know the article would be appearing. You were so keen to get the paper—'

'Because I thought there might be a report of the art show in it. Written by the editor.'

'No editor would spend his time doing write-ups of very minor local art shows.'

'I know that now. I suppose I was naïve to think he

would. You may not believe me, but I was set up, Brett.'

They were in the living room now, and Lauren sank wearily into a low chair. 'Will you listen if I explain?'

He stood, arms folded, his back to the stone fireplace. His whole demeanour conveyed repudiation of anything she might say in her own defence.

'Don't judge me before you've heard me,' she pleaded.

The movement of his hand invited her to continue, but she was sure he would listen with a closed mind.

She began with the clandestine conversation between Casey and his editor. Then she told him about the phone call from Harry Harper, and the implicit promise that he would write a piece about her as a young and gifted artist.

'And while I talked, Casey wandered round,' she finished.

'So?' Brett's voice was hard-edged, which had to mean that she had not got through to him. 'He couldn't have got very far with his snooping. Thanks to my father's obsession with locks and bolts, Talbert would have found both my bedroom and office barred to him. Did he by any chance go into the library and discover the secret room?'

'I'm sure he didn't. I wasn't that long on the phone.'

'Someone must have given him access to those wrecked paintings.'

'It wasn't me, Brett. You *have* to believe me.'

He regarded her, eyes half-closed, for a long time.

'Are you positive you made no mention to him of my writing activities?'

Lauren nodded. 'Positive. Except—'

His expression hardened again.

'Except I do remember telling him, when he asked me once where you were, that you had found an old typewriter and you were busy working in your room.'

'And you think it's possible,' he put in, 'that Talbert built on that statement?'

Miserably she nodded. 'I tried to cover it up. I said you were probably writing letters.'

He lifted a dismissive shoulder. 'All the same, that doesn't explain where he got the rest from.' He straightened. 'I'm going to my office.'

As he reached the stairs the telephone rang. He went to answer it. After all, Lauren argued silently, it's his house far more than it's mine.

'Hi, Elissa.' He sounded pleased, and Lauren's heart went into its usual sinking mode. 'Sorry to drag you from your tennis practice. When I called you earlier you were in class.' He listened for a while, then said, 'I tried to contact your mother. I rang the hotel, but she'd checked out. Yep, without telling me. Or you?' He sounded annoyed.

'Elissa, if you hear from her, will you give her this message? Will you tell her that I have to see her. It's vitally important that she comes to Old Cedar Grange as soon as she can make it. I want very much to see her.'

Now I know, Lauren thought dejectedly, why he didn't come straight back to the Grange from the newspaper office, and how Casey managed to get here first. He was telephoning his lady-friend, apparently desperate to make contact with her.

All of which showed, Lauren told herself, just how much Imogen Gard—and his daughter Elissa, however much he might deny the relationship—meant to him.

Casey arrived the next day, having offered to take Lauren and the commissioned paintings to her eager customers, one or two of whom lived quite far afield.

'I'm not surprised you sold so many during the art show,' Casey commented, carefully packing the pictures. 'These are good, Lauren. You'll make it big one day.'

'No thanks to you, your editor or your flaming newspaper,' she retorted acidly. 'I was promised a write-up, and by none other than the editor himself, but not a word about it appeared in any of the editions I read.'

'Mmm, sorry about all that.'

'That arranged phone call, you mean?'

'Well—' Casey's dismissive gesture was intended to deny its falseness.

'It's OK, I know I was used by you and Harry Harper,' Lauren declared. 'Casey.' He glanced up. She had deliberately softened her tone. 'As recompense for involving me so deeply in your shady journalistic investigations—and as a consequence ruining my—my friendship with Brett—will you tell me something?' He waited, expression closed and stubborn. 'Will you tell me who your sources really were?'

He paused for a long moment, then continued with the packing. 'We're nearly finished, aren't we? Let's carry them to my car.'

Lauren sighed irritably at his refusal to oblige.

'Before we go, Casey,' she declared angrily, 'there's something I'd like to say to you.'

'OK, shoot.'

'You asked for it.' Lauren fastened her jacket buttons one by one. 'I wish, Casey Talbert, that I'd never met you at Marie and Reggie's party. I wish— Oh, what's the use? The damage is done now. Let's do the rounds with my commissioned paintings, and then I want to go home.'

'Home? Don't you mean Brett Carmichael's home?'

'You do love turning the knife, don't you? But anyway, through your unscrupulous use of me in your desire for a scoop to further your career ambitions, it won't be my home for much longer.'

It was no use, Lauren couldn't settle to sleep. She thrust her legs out of bed and pulled on a silk robe.

Maybe a warm drink would help, she decided, and made for the corridor.

Just along from hers, she noticed that Brett's door was slightly ajar. Tiptoeing towards it, she heard a deep-throated moan which alarmed her so much that she went in.

Brett lay uncovered, his strong body gleaming with perspiration in the moonlight. Even as he lay there, still and unaware, she had to fight to stop herself from throwing her own body at his prostrate figure and begging him to love her.

As she watched, anxiety tensing her even more than her own restlessness had done, his arms lifted and fell. His head twisted on the pillow—first left, then right. She tiptoed over and felt his forehead. It burned beneath her hand. His eyes came open and he looked at her joylessly. No welcome here, she thought unhappily, only suspicion and doubt.

'The fever, Brett?' she whispered hoarsely. 'Has it come back?'

'I guess so,' was his dry-lipped answer. 'Water? Could you get me water?'

'Oh, Brett. . .' If all of her love was there in her voice for him to hear, she couldn't help it. 'I'll get you anything you want.'

She sped away, returning with a carafe and glass. She put her arms beneath him and lifted him so that he could drink, and this he did as if the liquid was nectar.

Again she went, returning this time with tepid water and a flannel. All this had happened the first time they'd met, she recalled, sponging him, loving his body, patting it dry. He would surely not now prevent her— now that they had shared the most intense intimacies that could exist between a man and a woman—from moving from his stomach down, down. . .

Ill as he was, he seized her wrist. 'Oh, no. And will you quit the fussing?'

'You want me to leave you alone?'

She put aside the bowl and towel, preparing to go, but his hand fastened on her arm.

'There's one thing,' he said harshly, 'that will help me over this. You—your body beside mine.'

She resisted, trying to free her arm. 'You don't know what you're saying. I'm your number one enemy, remember? I broke my promise and told the Press all about you...' If her bitterness showed, she didn't care any more.

He tugged her down. 'What matters to me at this moment is not your integrity, it's your warmth—'

'Of body, of course,' she said with a sting of sarcasm. 'As a spy and a cheat, I wouldn't possess any warmth of character, would I? After all, you're still convinced I betrayed you—'

'Traitor or not,' he returned grimly, 'at this moment I want you next to me.'

His words, Lauren thought despairingly, gave away the fact that he still believed she was capable of duplicity, but she did not resist the compelling strength of him for the simple reason that the place she most wanted to be was in his arms.

She lay beside him and he pulled her head down and round, pressing his lips to hers, prising hers open and probing mercilessly, as if he were intent on taking revenge for what he believed to be her betrayal of him. The kiss went on and on, until she had to drag the breath into her lungs.

'Brett...'

As he tore his mouth away from hers his name was dragged from the depths of her, and she found herself clinging to him, more in love with him, if that were possible, than ever.

In the night, almost unbelievably, a hand stroked her hair, lips touched her throat, a hand slid inside the robe to possess a breast.

He has the fever, she told herself. He's having vivid dreams and doesn't know what he's doing. He's need-

ing comfort—didn't he say so?—and in his restless
sleep he believes I'm Imogen Gard, the woman he
really loves.

Birdsong and daylight woke her. When she looked at
him she found him pale, but cool and rested. She—her
body—had been good medicine for him, which—and
she had to face reality—was the only reason he had
wanted her in his bed. And—she gently touched her
bruised mouth—to exact from her the revenge he felt
was his due after the betrayal of which he seemed so
sure she was guilty.

And there had been that phone call of his to Elissa,
hadn't there? His urgent and openly stated need for
her mother to come to him.

She loved him but Brett Carmichael was not for her,
Lauren Halstead. It was no good trying to pretend
otherwise, she told herself. He might make use of her
where his male appetites were concerned, but he did
not, and never would, love her.

She had retreated to her studio, and was idly and
somewhat desultorily flicking through the pages of a
book on birdlife, when the telephone rang.

Was it the call Brett had been waiting for? She held
back, giving him the chance to take it. The ringing
continued so she dashed down, lifting the receiver.

'Yes?' she queried, her tone strictly neutral. If it was
Imogen Gard, she would not be accused again of
impoliteness.

The caller cleared his throat. 'Is that Lauren—
Lauren Halstead?'

'It is.' She waited, wondering.

'Lauren, it's so long since I spoke to you—'

Brett came slowly down the stairs, poised as if to
take over.

'Mr Gard! M-Mr Gard?' A tingle of apprehension
ran over her.

Brett rested against the kitchen doorframe, his pale face growing paler. 'My father?' he asked gruffly. Lauren nodded. 'Ask him where he's calling from.'

This Lauren did, but she did not receive an answer.

'Will you tell me something, Lauren?' Redmund Gard asked. 'Are you alone in the house?'

'Do you mean, have I been living here alone? Well, no, Mr Gard, but—'

'Is it a man who is sharing the house with you?'

Oh, heavens, what was he thinking now? But then, wouldn't he be right? 'Yes, Mr Gard, but—'

'The answer to your earlier question, Lauren, is that I'm in London.' The phone went dead.

Lauren looked at Brett, lifting her shoulders. 'He's gone. He's in London.'

'Very specific,' was Brett's laconic comment.

'The question is,' Lauren said with a frown, 'where is he going from there? Here?'

'Oh, no. Now he knows you're not alone, he wouldn't want to intrude on your—shall we say—cosy arrangement.' He moved to the foot of the stairs. 'Or he might—just—have hazarded a guess that the man who is living here is me. In which case nothing—*but nothing*—would make him come to Old Cedar Grange. I've told you before, we are poison to each other.'

Lauren was horrified to think that after a gap of fifteen years Brett could put all thoughts of his father behind him, just like that. She shivered inside. If he could dismiss his father in such a callous way, how much would she, Lauren Halstead, matter to him—if at all—within a similar time-frame?

CHAPTER TWELVE

WHEN the scrape of tyres on the drive was followed quickly by the peal of the bell, Lauren was tidying her studio.

She and Brett almost collided on the landing.

'I'll go, if you like,' she offered. 'Just in case it's your f—'

'It won't be,' he said, then he was down the stairs and opening the front door as if the one person in the whole world he had wanted to see had come to him.

And hadn't she just? thought Lauren, returning slowly to her studio. She had watched Imogen step inside, fling her arms around Brett's neck and impel his head down so that her warm lips could reach his, imparting a long, impassioned kiss.

Worse than that, Lauren brooded, Brett had not seemed to object at all. His arms had gone round her, almost as if her kiss was what he'd been waiting for all his life.

'Darling,' Imogen had breathed, 'I got your message. You sent for me. I knew that one day you'd have to acknowledge that you couldn't live without me.'

The longer Lauren had witnessed this greeting—as though they had not met for years—the more intense her own agony had become.

She, Lauren, would have to face it; she'd have to leave. It was more than flesh and blood could bear, she agonised, to see the man she loved go so willingly and so unreservedly into another woman's arms.

There was the sound of cups and saucers being assembled in the kitchen, then chatter—talk drifting up of Elissa and her good progress at school. Their daughter, she thought joylessly. They have her and so much else in common. . .not to mention love.

'Lauren.' Brett's voice came up the stairs. 'Will you come down?'

She went to the door just in time to hear Imogen's objection to his invitation.

'Thanks,' Lauren responded, 'but I can make my own afternoon tea.'

'Lauren,' he repeated, tight-lipped, 'you'll join us.' It was a statement, almost an order.

'I'm busy.' She went to the top of the stairs. 'Your friend doesn't want me down there. If I can hear that, why can't you?'

In a few strides he was at the top of the stairs too, her wrist grasped by slightly cruel fingers. 'Do I have to drag you down?'

She went because she had to. 'What—what fantastic announcement are you going to make? Your engagement to the lady?' She tried vainly to free her wrist. 'If so, get another witness—not me. And if you don't know why—' to her horror, tears threatened '—then you're a th—thick-headed, d-dumb idiot.'

She was forced to follow him as if they were hand-cuffed together, but at last Brett released her, and Lauren was left ruefully rubbing her wrist.

Imogen, her expression superior and smug, was seated in the living room, and the low table bore only two poured cups of tea.

Her outfit was a dark two-piece, smartly tailored, her blouse of the palest pearly-pink. Pink, of course, the acid thought darted through Lauren's mind. It helps a woman look younger, doesn't it?

'No thank you to tea, I said,' Lauren told Brett. 'Please don't let me interrupt your cosy tête-à-tête.' She turned to leave, but Brett had positioned himself against the closed door.

'Take a seat, Lauren.'

There was something in his voice that made her do his bidding.

'Imogen.'

The woman paused in the act of taking a sip. 'Yes, darling?'

'You can drop the "darling" for a start.'

'What?' As she lowered her cup her hand shook tea all over the tray. 'What do you mean?' Her eyes, just a little scared, were on Brett now.

'You've read that report about me in the *News Journal*? About my past, my relationship with my father and—allegedly—with you? Not to mention the book I'm writing?'

'Well, yes, Brett, d—' She cleared her throat. 'Yes, I did. It was true, wasn't it—every wonderful word?'

Lauren looked from one to the other. Imogen's head was coquettishly on one side, and Brett, to Lauren, had never looked so hard, anger in every line of him.

The fever might have ebbed, but its effects still lingered in his pallor, the shadows around his eyes. Physically weakened or not, his brain was clearly working now—not sluggishly, but as that of a professional investigative journalist.

'I want you to tell me something, Imogen.' The woman's gaze fastened on him, flickered, then steadied. 'I want you to tell me, honestly and straightforwardly, the name of Casey Talbert's source for that story about me.'

She shook her head, lips parted as if gasping in wounded surprise at his question. '*I* tell you, Brett? How should I know?' She turned her stare onto Lauren. 'Ask *her*, Brett. You told me once that she knew everything. She found the letter, you said, and she discovered the secret room, found the paintings...'

'I've asked her, Imogen. In fact, I've actually accused her. She denies everything.'

'She would, wouldn't she?' Imogen's expression was venomous as she glared at Lauren.

'And you, Imogen, do you deny *everything*?' Brett spoke with deceptive softness, bringing Imogen's attention back to him.

Outside, the blueness of the sky had disappeared under the onslaught of heavy rain-bearing clouds. Not a glimpse of the sun was to be seen.

'Why, of course, d—Brett. Everything.'

'You would, wouldn't you?' The words, Imogen's words, had escaped Lauren's control, and sizzled like an indoor firework in the air of the living room.

'Keep out of this,' Imogen snapped, and to Brett, 'Send her away.'

'Don't worry. I'll go.'

Brett caught Lauren at the door, impelling her back to her chair.

'Do you want me to put pressure on you, Imogen?' He had taken up his old position by the door. She shook her head as if mystified. 'OK, I'll explain. Those generous amounts I've been paying regularly into your bank account to help towards Elissa's schooling, not to mention the financial help I give you, also—'

Imogen's hand went to her mouth, then she removed it to take in some tea, as if she needed to bolster her own sagging stamina.

Oh, no, Lauren thought, that really proves, doesn't it, that he *was* involved with her in the past, that the girl Elissa is indeed their daughter?

'Do you—' Brett pursued his quarry relentlessly as still she stared at him '—want me to give instructions to have those payments stopped?'

'Brett.' Imogen was pale now, her hands clasped tightly on her lap. 'What do you want me to tell you?'

'The truth, Imogen. The truth about everything. Start at the beginning. For instance, tell me the identity of Elissa's father—the name of the man you were living with at the time of her conception. Tell me why you fed my father so many lies, why you made it your business to alienate him from me to such an extent that he cut me out of his life.'

Imogen was leaning back now, looking her age and more, Lauren considered, and paler, if anything, than her questioner. She seemed to need the deep breaths she was taking, the cushion to support her head.

She took another long, shaky breath, then whispered, 'I'll tell you, Brett. But only if you send *her* away.'

Lauren rose at once.

'In the circumstances, Imogen,' Brett declared, '*I* make the conditions. Lauren stays.' He motioned her back to her chair. 'Now, Imogen.'

His jaw firmed, his eyes as hard as granite as they rested on the woman. They make me shiver, Lauren thought. Let alone the woman they're targeting.

'We—I—' She stood, swayed, and ran to Brett. 'It's no use, darling, I can't even find the words, unless—' she sought his eyes, which did not soften '—unless you hold me.' Her arms went round his neck and she pressed against him in a way so intimate that Lauren felt sickened.

Brett's arms lifted too, wrapping around Imogen's waist, and he rested his cheek on her hair. Lauren did not know how to hide her pain.

'That's better, darling,' Imogen said huskily against his chest. 'You want to know who my lover was at the time of Elissa's conception? And you want to know who her father was? One answer will suffice—*your* father, Ellis. *Your* father was both my lover and my husband, and therefore the father of my child.' Her head moved so that she could look up at him. 'Your half-sister.'

Lauren continued to stare through the window, noticing how the sun, having disappeared, emerged now and then from the cloud cover. So, she thought, Elissa is not Brett's daughter, after all. Yet her feelings were so numb she could scarcely take in Imogen's declarations.

Brett held Imogen away from him. 'Are you speaking the truth this time?'

Convulsively she pressed against him again. 'The truth and nothing but, Ellis. I swear.'

'So why did you tell my father those lies? That *I* was your lover and the father of your child? That I indulged in affair after affair—'

'Because you refused to be my lover, Ellis.'

'So it was a form of revenge, of retribution on your part?'

She nodded, pressing her frame harder than ever against him.

'One other thing,' Brett said, expression grim, 'who fed Casey Talbert with the rubbish he printed about me in that article of his? You?'

'You're quite merciless, Ellis. Yes, I did it,' she confessed in a whisper. 'I took him aside at the art show. I had taken the destroyed paintings from the secret room and stored them temporarily in my car to show him. He photographed them. The rest you can guess. Now, darling—' she pressed a kiss to his chest '—will you relent, after all this time?' She gazed up at him. 'Will you take me as your lover?'

As if he could not stand her nearness any longer, he thrust her from him.

'Do you know what you have done?' he responded harshly. 'You have caused misery and untold unhappiness to my father and myself. We've been alienated from each other for all these years because of your terrible lies. You have deprived Elissa of the knowledge of her true father and him of her company from birth to the present time. You owe us, Imogen, both my father and myself. It's time you paid the price.'

She was shaking now. 'Is that your final answer?'

'It is.'

Her body shuddered with suppressed sobs, but the look she turned on Lauren not only showed no remorse, it pierced her to the core.

'You think you've won, don't you?' she spat. 'But you haven't. This man won't stay in your life. He will leave you as he's left so many others.' Her eyes narrowed and her voice grew vicious as she flung her last warning in Lauren's face. 'Don't even begin to doubt it, Miss Halstead. *He will come to me in the end.*'

Lauren ran to the door. Brett moved to let her pass and she found sanctuary, but no peace, in her room.

Lying on her bed, Lauren listened to the rain. It had become prematurely dark in the half-hour she had lain there.

From downstairs she had heard raised voices, sobbing, sudden silences. What was Brett doing? Lauren wondered, twisted up inside. Forgiving Imogen, comforting her with words, kisses? Had Imogen won, after all?

Something made her go to the window. The rain had almost stopped and the cedar's heavy branches spread wide and dripped with the drops that had fallen on it.

The cedar tree...surely there was a figure beneath it? Of course it wasn't Brett's. He was in the living room, renewing his relationship with his lady-friend... wasn't he?

There *was* a man, so like Brett she could hardly believe it. She drew in a breath, let it out, then made for the stairs and thundered down them, bursting into the living room.

She didn't care what they were doing, whether they were in a clinch or... Imogen was standing with her back to the wall, her face blotchy with tears, her hair broken away from the chignon into which she had twisted it.

Brett was lounging against a chair-back, hands in pockets, his face grim but with a glint of satisfaction in his eyes.

Lauren ran past them both, struggling with the bolts on the double doors to the garden, flinging them wide.

There was a man, standing tall and thin and grey, and facially he was so like Brett that there was no mistaking his identity. Moving aside, Lauren gestured to Brett. He moved to investigate.

Imogen, nearer to the doors, saw the newcomer before he did. Recognition drew a gasping breath from her throat and she gave a piercing scream. Feverishly she gathered her belongings, running into the hall. Opening the front door, she hurled herself into the driveway, wrenched open her car door and roared away.

Brett kept on staring, stirring at last like someone waking from a deep sleep. He stepped into the semi-darkness, and as he neared the cedar tree the man in its shadow lifted his arms, then dropped them.

'Ellis.' One word, but there was a wealth of meaning in its sound. His arms lifted again, once again slowly returning to his sides. 'Do you forgive me?'

'Father—Father.' There was a catch in Brett's throat. 'It's been a long, long time.'

'Too long, son.' The newcomer's voice cracked at the word. 'Far, far too long.'

One more step and Brett's arms were round the older man, wrapping about him, holding him. They might have been statues, Lauren thought, frozen in time, turned to stone like the figures on their columns in the garden.

At last they broke apart, still staring at each other.

'The wasted years, Ellis,' Lauren heard the newcomer whisper. 'All those wasted years.'

There was a long, fraught pause. 'They're over, Father. They're behind us now.'

Brett picked up a suitcase and guided his father into the living room, and as they came into the light Lauren saw tears on the father's face, dampness on the son's.

Brett helped his father remove his rainproof jacket and sat him in the chair which Imogen had vacated.

Still they stared at each other, as if scarcely believing their eyes.

'Mr Gard—' Lauren began, then looked at Brett for guidance.

'I gather, Father, you've spoken on the telephone to my—' his smile was the warmest Lauren had seen for many days, and her heart danced '—my landlady.'

Lauren stared at Brett and their eyes clashed. You believe me now? hers were asking. You know I'm innocent of all your charges?

A step towards her, a smile that made her feel weak with joy, gave her the answer.

Redmund's laugh at his son's description of Lauren was as much a release of tension as amusement. The years which deep fatigue had added slipped away. His new-found happiness had renewed his vigour and put the colour back in his cheeks.

'I certainly have.' Then he sobered. 'Ellis. . .' His hand came out and it shook just a little. 'For fifteen or more years I have denied myself the pleasure of hearing you address me as Father. Oh, God—' his face paled again as the past came back to haunt him '—when I think of how you disappeared, or seemed to, off the face of the earth, how I tramped the globe looking for you. . .'

Lauren slipped from the room, pausing to dry her eyes before going to the kitchen to assemble more cups. She heard Brett leave the living room and go into the library, then return again to his father's side.

While the kettle came to the boil she sat at the table, arranging then rearranging cups and saucers on the tray.

When she rejoined them, having deferred the tea-making until a little later, Redmund was gazing at the painting of his first wife which Brett must have brought from the secret room. It was the only one of the three that had not been spoilt by the ruthless knife attack.

Now Redmund held the painting to his chest as if it were the most precious object in the world.

'Your mother, Ellis... I've seen her where she's living in Vancouver, and—I can hardly believe it myself—she is coming back to me. She married an invalid, nursed him until the end. Now she's free. Sh-she's never stopped loving me, Ellis.' His hands were shaking now. 'All those decades ago when she left, she still loved me, she said, and it took her years to recover from the shock.'

He shook his head, wiped his eyes with a handkerchief and pushed it back into his pocket. 'And I thought it was you, Ellis, who had poisoned her mind against me.' He shook his head.

'It was Imogen?' Brett queried, his voice thick with emotion.

'It was Imogen who told me lies about you. Imogen who told your mother I was having an affair with her—another lie—and that I wanted her, your mother, out of my life. You remember that Imogen was my secretary at the time? After your mother left me, I was devastated, but Imogen slowly slipped into the vacuum she had left.'

He looked down at the painting as if asking the forgiveness of the woman pictured there.

'Because my life without your mother was so empty—not to mention without you too, because I had sent you away—I fell for Imogen's apparent charms. Her comparative youthfulness appealed to me, and when my divorce from your mother came through, I proposed to Imogen.' He closed his eyes. 'For a while we were indeed man and wife, and I can totally accept that Elissa is my child.'

'And?' Brett prompted.

'And then,' Redmund went on, 'we began to drift apart. I was convinced Imogen had found someone else. It seems I was right, because she told me one day that she wanted a divorce—which, as you now know, I gave her.'

He held the picture of his first wife away, then held it to him again.

'That painting of you, Ellis—does it still exist?' Brett nodded. 'If only I hadn't defaced it.' Redmund sighed.

Brett stood by his father's chair. 'Were you aware, Father, that this—er—landlady of mine—' his smile swept over Lauren, and again her heart hit the heights '—is an artist? A good one.'

Redmund turned to her. 'This is true, Lauren?'

'I'm an artist, yes. But—' she smiled, lifting her shoulders '—good? I—'

She glanced at Brett, who held her eyes, and she could almost believe that his trust in her had returned. 'You know you are. False modesty, Lauren, doesn't help anyone in the art world make it big. About which, I seem to remember, you asked my opinion not so long ago.'

Lauren coloured and looked down at her hands. She felt rather than saw Redmund's speculative gaze on them.

'So, Lauren,' Redmund said, 'it would be possible, perhaps, for you to copy that painting of my son—without the—' He seemed unable to bring himself to utter the words.

'Without the defacement?' Lauren finished for him. She closed her eyes, visualising the portrait. 'It might be, Mr Gard. I think it could be done.'

Redmund stretched out his hand and Lauren rose to put hers into it. 'It would make me so very happy if you could, my dear.' He released her and leaned back. 'What a day this has been. A flight right across North America and the Atlantic. The journey here. The rediscovery of my son.' He paused. 'And the wonderful news that I also have a daughter.'

'Brett—I mean, Ellis told you?' His true first name felt strange on her tongue.

'While you were out of the room,' Brett put in.

'Fifteen years late,' Redmund added, 'but what does that matter? And, to cap it all, my phone call back to Canada to reassure myself that your mother, Ellis, has not changed her mind.' He levered himself tiredly from the low chair. 'She's packing her cases, she told me, and flying over to join me just as soon as she can book a flight.'

He paused. 'I bless the impulse that made me buy a British newspaper yesterday morning in Vancouver. I read a report some journalist had written about all that you'd been through, and about your being home, being here. . .'

Lauren and Brett exchanged glances. 'Does that mean—?' Lauren queried.

'That Casey Talbert syndicated his article to some of the nationals?' He nodded, but to Lauren's relief, the knowledge did not arouse his anger. 'At least,' he added with a touch of sarcasm, 'we have something to thank Talbert for.'

Redmund seemed to stoop under the weight of all the good news. A stride took his son to him, and he took his arm and supported him.

'You'll be staying here, Mr Gard?' Lauren asked, hurrying to the door to prepare a room for the visitor.

'My father insists on going to the hotel in the town, Lauren. He booked in there for the night.'

Lauren nodded. 'But one night only. Then you and your—' She glanced at Brett for his approval of her invitation. 'You and Brett's mother must stay here.'

'Thank you, my dear. Unless—' he chuckled '—we decide to have a second honeymoon alone together. After we have remarried, of course.'

Lauren was in her bedroom collecting her belongings into a pile on the floor when Brett returned from driving his father to the hotel.

He climbed the stairs and Lauren closed her eyes,

steeling herself for the sound of his footsteps taking him past her room.

'What the hell are you doing?' He was there in the doorway, staring at the mountain of clothes, books and ornaments. 'And where do you think you're going?'

'Away.' Her shoulders lifted and drooped. 'Wherever.' Her dull eyes met his. 'You won't need me here any more. Nor will your father. Or, when she arrives, your mother. There's no need for a house-sitter, is there?'

And, she thought, but did not add, when you patch up your quarrel with the woman you seem to have loved all these years, you'll be moving on too.

She glanced at him, wondering why he had not answered her question, then she really saw him. 'Brett, you look terrible.'

He shrugged off her sympathy. 'After-effects of the fever. It'll pass.' He turned wearily, then turned back, looking at her bed as if measuring the distance between where he stood and its inviting comfort.

Lauren rose swiftly. One of her arms went round his waist while the other closed over his forearm, and she led him towards the bed.

He managed the distance, collapsing full-length onto the covers and closing his eyes, then opening them again.

'Thanks for that.' His smile was plainly an effort. His lips quirked with the faintest touch of amusement.

'Was this—' he indicated the bed '—an invitation or an act of compassion?' In answer, her eyes overflowed with sympathy. 'It's pity. OK. I get the point. My attractions fade to nothing when compared with those of your journalist lover.'

'For heaven's sake, Casey's never been that. A friend, maybe, but—'

'You were close enough when I found him here the other day after I'd confronted him at his office. Practically entwined, would be a more accurate description.'

'If I told you I'd been using my so-called feminine wiles to get some information out of him—like who his sources were—would you believe me?'

'It would be so out of character for you—no is my answer.'

'Right. Then *I'm* saying—' she jerked to her feet '—that because you tolerated—almost seemed to enjoy—that clinch between Imogen and you when she was allegedly telling you the truth about what happened in the past, I'm beginning to believe Imogen's parting shot about you going back to her one day.'

Wearily he closed his eyes. 'If you're determined to believe that, how can I stop you? For as long as I've known her, Imogen's meant nothing to me.'

'So. . .' It hit her like a rifle-shot. . . She had guessed where her future lay.

He was a self-confessed wanderer, wasn't he? Which meant he'd go on his way unencumbered by any specimen of womankind. He might even pick one up on his route, wherever that might be, then drop her, find another, and another. . .

'Lauren.'

'Yes?'

'You can't leave. You've got a commission from my father. Repainting that portrait. You'll be well paid.' His eyes closed again.

When she went to the bed she could hardly believe her eyes. He was asleep, deeply so.

Oh, Brett, she thought, staring at his face so vulnerable in repose, the emotion she had held so forcibly in check overwhelming her, how I love you. It'll tear my heart from my body to go away, but how can I stay here now? She wiped her eyes with the back of her hand, but still the tears kept coming.

So we made love—no, she corrected herself, showing herself no mercy, we had sex. That's all it was for him, she lectured herself; the love in it was on my side only. She stifled a sob, but the next one tore at the air.

Her hand crept out, stroking his hair. For the last time she was touching him, then she'd pile her belongings into her cases and escape before he awoke, returning when he'd gone away for her painting gear.

Without warning his hand came up and captured hers, pulling her down beside him. He turned her towards him. He was fully awake now; no doubt about it.

'No, no, Brett.' She made to struggle. 'What's the use? When you've finished writing your book, you'll be on your way.'

'I will? Where?' His eyes glinted.

'Somewhere—anywhere. A wanderer like you gets restless, and—'

'Restless? Maybe—until he finds his journey's end.'

'But you told me once you had no intention of staying in this house any longer than was necessary.'

'True.'

'Which means—' she was puzzled by his half-smile '—that one day you'll pack up your computer and take to the road again.'

'Did I ever tell you what the "any longer than was necessary" condition meant?'

Eyes wide and wondering, she shook her head.

'As long as it took me to find—' He paused, waiting.

'The tranquillity of the soul you were looking for?'

'Lauren, look at me. At my eyes. . .into my eyes.' He held her chin, forcing her to do as he commanded. 'What do you see?'

Her mouth was so dry it resembled a desert. 'T-tranquillity? You found it?'

'It all depends.' He fingered her frown. 'On you, Lauren Halstead. Oh, God, Lauren.' He pulled her round and into his arms, and his eyes blazed into hers. 'Don't you see? *You* are my journey's end. From the moment I saw you, I knew I'd come home—really come home. Tell me something—a few minutes ago, when you thought I was asleep, you were crying. Why?'

Now was the time to tell the truth. 'Because—because I thought it was the end of the road. For you and for me. I thought you'd go away. I honestly thought you would go after Imogen and—'

'In a sense, it is the end of the road.'

Her heart sank and she tried to pull away.

'Journey's end—for both of us?' There was a catch in her voice, tears sprang. 'It—it would be such a pity—' her voice was thick '—because I love you, Brett. More than I can ever put into words, I love you.'

He groaned, his hands invading her cotton top, finding her breasts and moulding them. 'I was wondering how much longer I'd have to wait before I got it out of you. Shall I show you how much *I* love *you*? And then when I've shown you, we'll come up for air and talk about wedding dates. Right now we're going to make love—' He made to remove her top, but she stopped him.

'Your father, Brett—he'll have to be told.'

'He knows. I told him before I left him at the hotel.'

'Before you told me—*you told him*?'

'Why not? He was delighted. It made his day. And what a day he's had.'

The telephone shrilled and, accompanied by curses from Brett, Lauren dashed downstairs to answer it.

'Marie? *Marie.* How good to hear from you. You'll never believe—'

But Marie had her own news to impart. 'Reggie and I, we're getting married,' she announced excitedly. 'We're returning home for the wedding.'

'Well, then,' Lauren put in triumphantly, 'you'll be able to come to *our* wedding too.'

'*Your* wedding? For goodness' sake, Lauren, who are *you* marrying? Say it's not Casey.'

'It's not Casey. It's Brett.'

She could almost see Marie's frown. 'Brett? Brett who?'

'Well, Ellis, then.'

'Two men? You've got to be joking, Lauren.'

'No—one, of course.'

'Hey, you don't mean *Ellis Gard*?'

'I do. It's a long story, Marie. I'll tell you one day.'

'That's great news. Must go. I'll call again some time—with dates and so on. Bye.'

Brett was pulling her back down beside him when the doorbell clanged.

'For God's sake,' Brett exploded, and again to the accompaniment of Brett's curses Lauren scuttled down the stairs.

'Casey! Hi.' He made to enter, but she kept the door half closed. 'If you're wanting a story,' she told him, eyes brilliant with happiness, 'is there a scoop at Old Cedar Grange!' She counted on her fingers. 'It's about the return of a father and his reconciliation with a long-lost son. The discovery by the father of a daughter and by the son of a half-sister. The unmasking of a villain—feminine not masculine, and she's no lady! And an attack of fever. Plus about five happy endings.'

'What's going on down there?' Brett appeared at the top of the stairs. 'Talbert? Either you print a retraction and an apology regarding those outrageous lies you and your editor printed about me and mine, or I'll sue the hide off both of you for libel. Lauren, shut him out and come back to bed.' He walked away.

Casey's eyes almost came out of their sockets. 'Bed? You—and him?' He almost choked over the words.

'To get the story, Casey—' Lauren was enjoying herself '—you'll have to interview the man at the centre of it all.' Her finger pointed up the stairs. 'And this time you'd better get your facts right. He's a professional, like you, but far better at it.' She went to close the door but then changed her mind, opening it again. 'If you do as you've been told, I might—just might—invite you to my wedding.'

Brett met her at the bedroom door, closing it, turning the key and pushing it into his jeans pocket.

'Thank God for my father's compulsion for locks on doors,' he said. 'If the phone rings it'll be unanswered. If there's a caller at the door there'll be no one to let them in. You get me?'

Her heart bursting with happiness, Lauren nodded. 'Oh, Brett—' her arms lifted to his neck '—I love you so.'

'So show me.' He peeled her top over her head, kissing her breasts one by one. 'So tell me with your body. . .'

'And you,' she said breathily as he lifted her and lowered her to the bed. 'Show *me*, darling. . .'

His mouth prevented her from saying more, moving over her lips, her throat and down to breasts that rounded still more in response to the caresses of his tongue.

Soon she was naked beside his unclothed body, and she loved the sight of his muscled strength, his legs which wound around her own, his chest with its dark mat of hair so soft against her cheek.

With his palms and tongue and teeth he was causing a swamping ache to her loins and a pulsing throb to her womanhood as his mouth and hands found their way to the most intimate of places, bringing a choked gasp to her throat.

Then he took her, and she arched at the hardness of him inside her, never wanting his thrusting possession to stop, crying out his name and her love for him as, at long last, they reached the crowning moment in insurpassable, faultless harmony.

'So, my love,' he murmured against her breasts some time later, 'you will replace your belongings where they've been since you moved into this house. And from today on you will move into my bedroom. Right?'

'Right,' she echoed, her hand on his thigh.

His eyes softened as they stared into hers. 'Those eyes of yours,' he said huskily. 'A guy could lose himself in them. All sense of time, of reality. . .'

'That's what Mitch said,' Lauren commented with a smile.

A deep frown furrowed Brett's forehead. 'Who the hell's Mitch?'

Her smile deepened, a little leap of pleasure nudging her heart at the way instant jealousy had gripped him.

'An old boyfriend. It's OK—' she reached up and kissed his chin '—I ditched Mitch.'

A laugh took away the frown. 'For a minute I thought I had another rival. Know something? When I was in captivity—' his finger ran down her cheek '—I used to fantasise about a girl like you. . .eyes dreamy, full of warmth and love, and a figure—' his hands traced her shape, lingering over her breasts, then moving down '—like a pocket Venus.'

She frowned, stroking his hair. 'That fever you were left with—will it keep recurring for the rest of your life?'

A shoulder lifted and her lips pressed against it. 'It might, but it soon passes. There's one fever, though, that will affect me to my dying day.'

Concerned, she moved slightly away. 'What kind of fever?' she asked. 'Is it serious?'

'Very serious.' His finger smoothed away her frown. 'It's the fever I feel rising inside me every time I look at you. And there's only one cure for that, beloved, and that is you. Know something else? That fever's coming on me right now.' He reached for her again. 'And this is the cure that I'll need for evermore.'

'Isn't it lucky,' she declared, sliding back into his arms, 'that I like the cure as much as you do?'

MILLS & BOON®

Next Month's Romances

♡

Each month you can choose from a wide variety of romance with Mills & Boon. Below are the new titles to look out for next month in our two new series Presents and Enchanted.

Presents™

Enchanted™

Available from WH Smith, John Menzies, Volume One, Forbuoys, Martins, Woolworths, Tesco, Asda, Safeway and other paperback stockists.

MILLS & BOON®

We value your comments!

Please spare a few moments to fill in the following questionnaire.
NO STAMP NEEDED.

Last month we introduced two new cover designs for our romance novels—Presents and Enchanted—and we'd like to know what you think. Please tick the appropriate box ☑ to indicate your answers.

---

1. How long have you been a Mills & Boon Romance reader?

Less than 1 year ☐   1-2 years ☐   3-5 years ☐
6-10 years ☐   Over 10 years ☐

2. How many Mills & Boon Romances do you read/buy in a month?

	Read	Buy
1-4	☐	☐
5-8	☐	☐
9-12	☐	☐
13-16	☐	☐
Over 17	☐	☐

3. From where do you usually obtain your Mills & Boon Romances?

Mills & Boon Reader Service ☐
WH Smith/John Menzies/Other Newsagent ☐
Supermarket ☐
Borrowed from a friend ☐
Bought from a second-hand shop ☐
Other (please specify) _____

*4. Thinking about the **Presents** cover do you:*

Like it very much ☐   Don't like it very much ☐
Like it quite a lot ☐   Don't like it at all ☐

Please turn over ☞

5. Thinking about the **Enchanted** *cover do you:*

Like it very much ❑   Don't like it very much ❑

Like it quite a lot ❑   Don't like it at all ❑

6. *Do you have any additional comments you'd like to make about the Presents and Enchanted covers?*

_____

_____

7. *It is intended that the two new covers will help readers to distinguish between the different types of romantic storylines, do you think this is a good idea?*

Yes ❑   No ❑

8. *Are you a Reader Service subscriber?*

Yes ❑   No ❑

9. *Please indicate your age group*

16-24 ❑   25-34 ❑   45-54 ❑   55-64 ❑   65+ ❑

Thank you for your help

Please send your completed questionnaire to:

Harlequin Mills & Boon Ltd.,
Presents/Enchanted Questionnaire,
Dept. M, FREEPOST, P.O. Box 183,
Richmond, Surrey, TW9 1ST

P1

Ms/Mrs/Miss/Mr _____

Address _____

_____

————————— Postcode —————————

You may be mailed with offers from other reputable companies as a result of this application. If you would prefer not to receive such offers, please tick box. ❑